MOMENTS FOR YOU

THE WILDER BROTHERS

CARRIE ANN RYAN

MOMENTS FOR YOU

A WILDER BROTHERS NOVEL

By

Carrie Ann Ryan

MOMENTS FOR YOU
A Wilder Brothers Novel
By: Carrie Ann Ryan
© 2024 Carrie Ann Ryan

Cover Art by Sweet N Spicy Designs
Photo by Wander Aguiar Photography

PRAISE FOR CARRIE ANN RYAN

"Count on Carrie Ann Ryan for emotional, sexy, character driven stories that capture your heart!" – Carly Phillips, NY Times bestselling author

"Carrie Ann Ryan's romances are my newest addiction! The emotion in her books captures me from the very beginning. The hope and healing hold me close until the end. These love stories will simply sweep you away." ~ NYT Bestselling Author Deveny Perry

"Carrie Ann Ryan writes the perfect balance of sweet and heat ensuring every story feeds the soul." - Audrey Carlan, #1 New York Times Bestselling Author

"Carrie Ann Ryan never fails to draw readers in with passion, raw sensuality, and characters that pop off the page. Any book by Carrie Ann is an absolute treat." – New York Times Bestselling Author J. Kenner

"Carrie Ann Ryan knows how to pull your heartstrings and make your pulse pound! Her wonderful Redwood Pack series will draw you in and keep you reading long into the night. I can't wait to see what comes next with the new generation, the Talons. Keep them coming, Carrie Ann!" –Lara Adrian, New York Times bestselling author of CRAVE THE NIGHT

"With snarky humor, sizzling love scenes, and brilliant, imaginative worldbuilding, The Dante's Circle series reads as if Carrie Ann Ryan peeked at my personal wish list!" – NYT Bestselling Author, Larissa Ione

"Carrie Ann Ryan writes sexy shifters in a world full of passionate happily-ever-afters." – *New York Times* Bestselling Author Vivian Arend

"Carrie Ann's books are sexy with characters you can't help but love from page one. They are heat and heart blended to perfection." *New York Times* Bestselling Author Jayne Rylon

Carrie Ann Ryan's books are wickedly funny and deliciously hot, with plenty of twists to keep you guessing. They'll keep you up all night!" USA Today Bestselling Author Cari Quinn

"Once again, Carrie Ann Ryan knocks the Dante's Circle series out of the park. The queen of hot, sexy, enthralling paranormal romance, Carrie Ann is an author not to miss!" *New York Times* bestselling Author Marie Harte

MOMENTS FOR YOU

Two widows. One wedding dress. And a promise of forever in the next installment of the Wilder Brothers from NYT Bestselling Author Carrie Ann Ryan.

A wedding dress is meant to be worn only once.

When a stranger finds herself in need of a miracle at the last minute, I do the unthinkable: I offer mine to her.

The same one I wore down the aisle for my late husband.

Now I'm invited to the wedding and finding myself wondering why I shut myself away from the world for so long.

I'm only meant to be at the Wilder Retreat for a single day except I go home with not only a job offer, but the promise of something more.

Ridge Wilder is hiding secrets of his own. And the undeniable chemistry between us burns before we even contemplate taking that first step.

Only I've already had my happy ever after. I never planned on finding another.

And Ridge is even far more broken than I am—with a past that might come back to haunt us both.

CHAPTER ONE

RIDGE

As a man who's seen things, has lived through the worst and suffered through the rest, I couldn't believe I worked at a place that hosted weddings for a living. Actual weddings, with tulle and lace and cake. The amount of work that went into weddings seemed to grow with each passing day and while I was glad I wasn't in charge of it, I was confused how it all worked and why I was on the periphery of it.

It'd been two years since I moved to the outskirts of San Antonio, Texas, and I still woke up every morning wondering how the hell I'd scored my job. Because it didn't really feel like my job. People got married, looked happy, and went off to live happily ever after, leaving me doing God knows what in the background.

And somehow my growly ass was part of it.

Still not quite sure where I fit in.

"Why are you growling?"

I looked over at my boss, Trace, and shook my head. I was damn lucky that Trace had been looking for someone to help him with the security side of the Wilder Retreat. I'd had my own job a few hours away and thought I knew what the fuck I was doing.

Then fate had decided that no, that was not the case. No, my life turned on its axis, and there was no coming back from that.

When me and my brothers came here for a family reunion, I had offered myself up as tribute. I needed a job, a change. A place to run away, and I hadn't wanted to ask my cousins, the ever popular and successful Wilder brothers, for help.

They owned this retreat. They, along with their spouses, had taken an old inn and winery that had slowly been going downhill and created something that was quite stunning.

Even when the storm knocked out some of the walls, had demolished a building or two, and carved through the land nearly two years ago, they rebuilt.

Because that's what happened when the Wilders got in the way. We looked at the destruction, tried to fight back, and then we rebuilt.

And somehow I joined the fray, dragging along my three brothers.

Although Gabriel didn't stay here, as he was usually out on tour being a rockstar, he was still here as much as he could be.

Brooks had decided to come and help rebuild because that's what his job was, and he decided to stay. Same with Wyatt. Although Wyatt had decided to go crazy and built a bar and distillery on the property even though there was already a damn winery. Apparently the Wilder brothers and cousins were becoming a conglomerate, and I was the security specialist.

Because of course that made sense.

"Ridge? What's up with you?"

I shook my head, pulling myself out of my own thoughts. The anniversary of my coming here was quickly approaching, and that meant in six months I'd reach the anniversary of something I didn't want to think about. So I wouldn't.

"What? I'm fine."

"Sure, you are. Do you want to talk about it?"

"I blame you marrying Elliot and Sidney for you thinking I actually want to talk about my feelings. Elliot is the cousin who always likes to do that."

Trace shook his head, a small smile playing on his face. He'd shaved his beard off a few months ago, and I knew my cousin had mourned that the big bushy thing was gone. But Trace liked a clean face, and it still surprised me to see that strong jawline instead of the beard.

I loved that my boss and cousin had not only gotten married, but they also married someone they had met on the property, a woman left at the altar. Well, she sure knew how to show the world that she could stand on her own two feet. Because she married not one man, but two, right on this property nearly a year and a half ago.

In fact, all of my cousins were married. The only female Wilder of our generation was married with two kids up in Colorado but visited often. Eliza was brilliant, and one of my favorite people in the world. I was also glad she didn't live here so she couldn't ask me any questions. She'd be able to see right through my snark and growls. And while I knew my cousins and brothers all wanted to know why I had decided to move here seemingly out of the blue, I knew Eliza would be the only person I would break for.

Eli was the eldest of us all. The fact that he was in charge of this whole place and seemed to have a vision for the Wilder Retreat and Winery to grow into something huge, honestly didn't shock me. It should have, but it hadn't. All six of my male cousins had gone into the military, kicked ass, and when things had broken down, or they were forced out, they came together because they needed each other. Now they all seemed healthy, happy, married.

Eli and his wife Alexis had a daughter named Kylie; and Evan and Kendall, who had been married twice, had twins, Reese and Cassie.

The rest of my cousins were probably going to follow the others when it came to babies, but for now they were taking time to enjoy being married.

I was kind of grateful for that—not that I wanted to think about it, because that would just etch those thoughts on my face, and then people would have questions.

And I hated questions.

"Come on, let's go do the perimeter. We have the team on, but thankfully we don't have a wedding today."

I rolled my shoulders back, glad Trace changed the subject. No one needed to know why I started working here, why I needed to be near family.

Nobody.

"I thought we had that retirement ceremony?" I asked, looking over my tablet.

Trace nodded as we headed out of his office, in the

main building of the inn, situated in the center of the Wilder property, and down the stairs.

It was part of the original structure, though some of it had been damaged in the tornado. They had rebuilt, thanks to my brother Wyatt, and everything was starting to look up again. Since my cousins bought the place, they had revamped many of the cabins on the property and added a few more in the distance that were eco-friendly. I was grateful for that, considering I lived in one. They also added a spa, which made me snort and roll my eyes, but people liked it, and the infinity pools were nice to swim in when no one was around. I didn't want to deal with people.

That's why I loved my job. I protected people, but I didn't have to talk to them to do it.

They'd also added a high-end restaurant down the hill near the entrance of the property. My cousin-in-law Kendall ran it, as well as the catering and restaurant on the property itself, and I wasn't quite sure how she was doing it all. Her longtime sous chef had moved away over a year ago because Sandy's partner had gotten a dream job in Paris.

I didn't quite understand how my cousin-in-law did it all, but she did kick ass. And the restaurant served some of the best food I'd ever had in my life. A little high-end for me, considering I wasn't used to having at least three forks and two knives at a place setting, or having someone clean up the crumbs between each serving. Made me feel like I had too many thumbs.

Kendall was on her third round of sous chefs because people couldn't keep up with her. And I didn't say that lightly. Kendall could kick ass and expected the best out of people. And the people she kept hiring looked on paper as if they knew what they were doing, and passed all the security checks, but they sucked.

One had only wanted to be near another cousin-in-law of mine, an Academy Award-winning actress, and our other cousin-in-law, who happened to be the most famous pop star in the world. Oh, they had gone to culinary school, and were amazing at cooking and creating pastries for events and the restaurant, but they had spent most of their time trying to stalk both Lark and Bethany.

Kicking them out had been fun.

At least it gave me a little thrill.

The second person couldn't keep up with the demand of a wedding business, catering business, and a high-end restaurant.

It was a lot, but Kendall had it down to a science, and she just needed someone to step in who could not only follow rules but have some vision when it came to baking.

Of course, it didn't always work out that way.

She was on the third one now, and I thought they were doing pretty good, considering some of the desserts I'd tried, but knowing our luck, I wasn't sure how long they would last.

"Are we heading out to the winery today?" I asked, following Trace.

The property itself had come with the vines and the winery. Many of the staff working on that had actually come with the original place too. They were okay with the change to Wilder Wines and were damn good at creating new blends.

Two of my cousins were handling that section, which was good because I wasn't a wine guy, though they made things taste pretty decent.

"On our end, we have two tours going on today, bigger ones with the wine clubs, but the team has it. You and I are going to go head over to the west side and check on the bar and distillery." Trace rolled his eyes. "I still cannot believe that Wyatt somehow convinced the others to add that on."

I laughed; I couldn't help it.

"Well, we Wilder cousins couldn't just stand back and let the six of them take over the world."

"Much to Elliot's consternation," Trace added. "However, you guys buying the acreage next door and buying in to the business so you're all partners? Damn good decision. Although I still don't know why you call me boss when you're part owner."

I shook my head, that odd uncomfortable feeling coming again. This place had become far more permanent than I planned, but I couldn't help it. My brothers were here. My family was here.

And I didn't have anywhere else to go.

"You own it, too, just like Elliot does. Apparently it's an all-in-the-family situation. And you were here first for security."

"Good job I've done." He rolled his eyes. "I swear, people are getting more brazen."

"But you're keeping them out. Keeping people safe. I know it's not easy when this place has become a hotspot for celebrities to get married and have events. Although why they would want to come to San Antonio, Texas, I don't know."

Trace snorted and looked over his shoulder, as if afraid someone would pop out of the bushes and kick me in the shins for saying that. "You do realize that we live here now. We should probably not shit on the city we live in."

"True. And we are in hill country. It's beautiful. But, I don't know, I thought most people would want a destination wedding on a beach or something."

"But then sand gets in places." Trace shuddered, and I threw my head back and laughed, truly meaning it.

I liked Trace. I liked it here.

We had over a hundred acres with a winery, a distillery, a spa, forested trails, and cabins. We had a tasting room, barrel rooms, and huge buildings for all the equipment for the winery. Let alone the vines.

We had a farmhouse, chicken coops, and even another annex with all the farm equipment. We had an outside dance hall, an indoor one, and a huge fountain area for parties and weddings.

I literally couldn't believe this was where I lived, and this was what we did for a living. I watched people make promises to each other and wondered what would have happened if I'd been able to keep mine.

"I don't know what we're going to do," Alexis snapped as she paced down the path, Eli on her heels.

"Babe. Let's go inside and talk about it. We'll figure it out."

She whirled on him, though I saw panic in her eyes, not anger. "Figure it out? How the hell are we supposed to figure it out when I'm the one freaking out? I never freak out. I'm the wedding planner for this entire business. I can handle this. I've handled everything. But I don't know if I can do this, Eli."

She pulled her long dark hair away from her face, putting it in a messy bun, which I'd rarely seen from her. She was the epitome of being put together. I had seen brides break down, mothers-in-law fighting over their precious children, and even people coming to blows, and Alexis had always been steadfast.

She could handle anything, and yet for some reason, something seemed to have broken her.

"Babe. We can figure this out." Eli cupped his wife's face. People were milling about, guests who were here just for a vacation rather than a wedding, but nobody was paying attention. They all had things on their minds, nothing to do with the tableau in front of them.

Trace and I went to them, knowing that this might be private, but if she was freaking out, we had to find out if it was for security reasons.

"I don't know why I'm acting like this," Alexis whispered.

"We both know why you're acting like this."

The two of them met each other's gazes, and I knew.

I ignored the little clutch in my belly, the memories.

Because they didn't matter. Why should they?

Enough time had passed.

It wasn't as if anything had really been real, right? I

stood on that precipice before, watched the unending worry and hope and promises cascade into my life.

But it wasn't there anymore.

I worked in the business of protecting futures, so why should I live in the past?

"Everything okay over here?" I asked, my voice low. I needed to get out of my head, needed to forget. But when the two of them looked at me, their eyes wide, it was a kick in the gut.

"Sorry. Just overreacting." Alexis wiped away her tears. I hated seeing them because Alexis didn't cry. Not when it came to work. She kicked ass.

"What's wrong? Do you need to sit down?" Trace asked.

Both Eli and Alexis looked at each other before they smiled a secret smile, and I ignored the pain in my stomach and the way my palms went damp.

I ignored it all.

"There's a bride issue, and I'm overreacting, you know, because hormones." She grinned as she said it, her eyes brightening. Eli's chest puffed out. I nearly rolled my eyes at the sight, until I remembered.

I remembered doing the exact same fucking thing.

"Well damn," Trace said before he reached out and plucked Alexis off her feet. He whirled her about as she laughed and Eli scowled. "Hands off my wife. You already have two spouses of your own. Don't hurt her."

"As if I could hurt her. Look at you, congratulations to you both." Trace smacked a hard kiss on her lips, and Eli continued to scowl, though I saw the pride and happiness in his gaze.

"We were waiting until we got out of the first trimester. But yes, there's going to be a new Wilder."

"Shudder the thought," I said with a laugh. "But you know the world needs more Wilders."

Did my voice sound as if I was happy? Could they hear the hollowness? The rasp?

I didn't think so, not with the absolute glee on their faces, so I just ignored the feeling in my stomach. Ignored the idea that I wanted to jump from the nearest hill and see what could happen to a body once bones broke and the world ended.

But I wasn't that man. I couldn't be. I had to be here.

Even though I wanted to be anywhere else.

"Seriously though, congratulations," I added after clearing my throat. "But what else is wrong? Something with a wedding?"

Alexis nearly teared up again, and I cursed myself.

Then she did the most amazing thing and rolled her

shoulders back and pulled out her phone. "We lost a dress."

Trace whistled through his teeth as Eli winced and I just looked confused.

"As in you misplaced it? Want me to ask the guys to look for it? I'm sure we can find it. Or do you think it was stolen? Hell, please don't tell me it was stolen right under our noses?"

I didn't even want to think about the paperwork and publicity with that shit.

Alexis immediately shook her head, but the relief was only short-lived. "The bride was wearing a family heirloom, her great-grandmother's dress. Her grandmother and her mother had each worn it, and they each did small alterations just for the fit. They went to a reputable seamstress, though not one on our list of vendors. They went to the same place they had always used. Or so they thought." Alexis scowled, and I winced. I would not want to be on the receiving end of that look. "It seems that it's the same building, the same name, but not run by the same person. That person closed down shop and took everything. No notes, no calls, and are completely unreachable. They took all of the dresses, and I can't find them. And I can usually find anyone."

"Are you kidding me?" I asked, shaking my head. "Did they call the cops?"

Alexis nodded. "Over twenty dresses are gone, probably more. Only one from here, but there are countless brides out there who are in pain because they lost their dresses, and this one was an heirloom. I don't know what the ever loving hell we're going to do. The wedding is in three days, and we don't have a backup dress." She put her hand on her stomach before going slightly green and twisting towards the bushes.

Eli was immediately at her side, holding her hair back as I jogged over to the side building and plucked out a bottle of water that we had in one of the fridges for all of the staff and guests.

I came back and unscrewed the top, handing it over.

She nodded her thanks.

"Oh good, why do I always get second-trimester nausea?" she asked before she gulped half the bottle of water down.

I remembered another person who had that same thing, though I wouldn't think about it. Or I kept lying to myself that I wouldn't.

"What are you going to do?" I asked, oddly curious. Because Alexis was a problem solver, but I didn't know how they were going to solve this.

"I can't bring back the memories, I can't fix what

was lost, but maybe I can do something else. I just hope asking for help works."

She nodded and headed back to her office, looking for all the world like the empress on a war mission. Eli nodded at us and followed her. Trace pulled out his phone, and I wondered if he was calling his contacts to see if there was something he could do.

I wasn't sure what I could do to help, since this was completely out of my comfort zone. But she was right, we couldn't fix the past. We could only look to the future.

And I wasn't good at that. Never had been.

That's why I lived here. Away from things that reminded me of my past.

But I guess that wasn't quite the case.

Because when you watch the woman you love die, feel her last heartbeat under your hands, you know that there's no hope for a future. Especially when she was carrying your child.

You don't get second chances. You don't get happy ever afters. I could watch others do so around me, but it wasn't for me.

I had that. And I lost it.

I lost everything.

I never wanted a second chance.

At least not unless I could turn back time.

CHAPTER TWO

AURORA

I hadn't exactly pulled myself out of the darkness —I had slowly rolled back into the abyss, climbed up the hill, rocketed back down, and found myself on a dirt path that didn't go anywhere. It wound to and fro, up and down. Sometimes there were stairs, hand hewn and a little rickety. Some were made of stone, a little stronger, more stable. I knew those stones came from the people before me, that club I never wanted to join.

Grief was overwhelming and yet nearly invisible.

Grief stabbed and stole and lied and shouted and whispered.

Grief hid and jumped out of the darkness and waited to do it again.

Grief rocked me to sleep and woke me up.

Grief was never ending, and yet it didn't stab as sharply as it once had.

At least most days.

Today marked five years since I lost everything. Since darkness had taken my light.

Five years since I lost William, and everything changed.

I didn't like the word widow. And yet I clung to it because it was the only connection I had left to William. I didn't want to be *just* a widow though. To have people look at me and know what I lost and show their pity in their eyes and their actions. When they found out I was alone and there was that pause before they said anything else. An awkwardness would settle in because how long was too long to grieve? And then they would clear their throats and say they were sorry and you would move on with the conversation. You had to assure them you were okay. That yes you were sad, and yes he would always be part of your life, but you didn't want that to be the only thing to define you.

You needed to make your grief about them, so they were comfortable remembering who you were, and not just who you were without your husband.

I was thirty-one years old. Thirty-one years old and had been a widow for five years.

"I miss you, baby," I whispered into the silence, even though I wasn't sure I believed he could hear me.

I had never allowed myself to think about what lay beyond this world. I thought of the afterlife as this wibbly wobbly timelessness that I would figure out when I was older and things made sense.

I would worry about the ever after once I got a little more settled into my happy ever now.

That's what William and I had always told ourselves. We were in our twenties. We were young and happy and had the rest of our lives together. We were thinking about children and what we would do on our first real vacation, now that we had a few bucks to spare. We had saved and scrimped and done our best to start the next phase of our life in our late twenties. People thought we'd gotten married too young, and while my family had been all for it, loving William, William's family hadn't been thrilled. Their son had been too young to settle down with the likes of me.

I rolled my eyes at that, still annoyed.

It wasn't their fault they didn't understand me, but everything else they had done afterward was their fault. I was grateful William wasn't here to see what they had done. Who they had become. But maybe that wibbly wobbly afterlife meant he saw everything.

Maybe he saw me here now, sitting in my sweats on

the couch, feeling sorry for myself because I was all alone.

William would've wanted me to buck up, get my act together, and work.

He would also want me to live, to take chances, to make mistakes. To become the epitome of Ms. Frazzle and get messy.

"Knock knock," a familiar and welcome voice said from my front door as she took it upon herself to walk in without asking, smiling brightly. A little too brightly, but I wasn't going to mention it.

Joni, my best friend and confidante, came inside, a bottle of wine in one hand and a covered dish in the other.

"I would have brought you cake or cookies or something, but we both know that you can bake anything far better than I could, or even what I could get at the store." She set both of her items on the table in front of me and put her hands on her hips.

"So. Did you shower today?"

I raised a brow, then looked down at my sweats. "Oddly yes. These are my work sweats. They don't even have stains on them yet. I'm practically fancy."

She gave me a soft smile and my lips wobbled, but I ignored it. I wasn't going to let it affect me. I was going to be fine today. Everything was going to be okay.

Nothing had changed from the day before, nor would it change tomorrow. William would still be gone, and I would still be left behind. I would just carry these scars on my heart, and a few on my back.

After all, I'd been in the car with him. The one behind the wheel. I heard his scream, echoing with my own, and then I remember being pulled out, but William not coming with me. That's all I remembered of that day, which was odd because most people said they remembered the day that their husband died in such vivid detail that it followed them into their dreams.

But I didn't dream of that. No, I dreamed of everything from before, and everything that came after.

Because so much came after.

"You're allowed to cry, you know. You're allowed to have this whole bottle of wine, or eat that entire green bean casserole that I know you love, or you can work, watch TV—you could do anything. The one requirement I had for you was to shower. Because that's what you wanted me to ask of you. You see? You're already surpassing your expectations."

"As long as you don't call me a strong, confident woman that is handling grief in a wonderful way, we're doing dandy."

Joni winced. "Please tell me the neighbor that shall

not be named did not say that to you."

I stood up and went to the covered dish, grateful my friend seemed to understand me more than I did.

"Oh yes. Complete with a heartfelt apology that her husband was out mowing the lawn this morning. Because the fact that her husband was alive might hurt me or something." I rolled my eyes and went to the kitchen to get two spoons.

"At least you moved out of your other house and started over here, because this kitchen is the most amazing thing I've ever seen." She sighed. "My God, Aurora, do you want me to kick her ass? I'm pretty sure I could do it. She's mostly just spite and sinew."

I raised a brow as I handed over a spoon and Joni pointed to the wine bottle. "Interested?"

I shook my head. "No, I have a work order to do. I'm just waiting for the cookies to cool." I gestured towards my workstation and all the prep work that had taken over my morning. "How about sparkling water? That sounds good, right?"

"Anything you want," Joni said, and I could feel her eyes on me.

She was just as worried about me as my family was, but from her it didn't feel like pity, or desperation for everything to be normal, even though there wasn't such a thing as normal. Oh, they could call it the new normal. They could call it whatever they wanted, but it was never the same.

"Did you talk to your parents today?" she asked. I nodded, pouring us each a glass of sparkling water. I pulled my long, dark hair away from my face, aware that though I had washed it and blown it out, it was going to end up with a kink in it anyway from being in a ponytail or bun for most of the day. I didn't ice cookies with my hair in my face. That was just asking for a food code violation and unhappy clients.

"Yes, this morning before they went to work. They didn't bring it up, they just wanted to hear my voice. I am not sure if I should call this an anniversary, or just a day."

"Have you talked with William's family?" I took a large drink of my water, then shook my head before I dug into the green bean casserole, aware that I would probably eat this whole dish if it were up to me.

"Good. They're assholes."

I swallowed the yummy mushroom creamy green bean goodness and shrugged. "They miss their son. I don't know why they would talk to me."

"Because you were a part of their son's life. For nearly a decade."

"High school sweethearts that turn into husband and wife don't actually equate to their son's forever.

They only want to remember the good parts. They don't want to remember that I was part of those good parts. I'm just the woman that survived the car wreck."

"That a drunk driver caused."

"And I was driving," I said and ate another bite.

It hadn't mattered that the drunk driver had crossed three lanes of traffic to hit us head on. It hadn't mattered that the driver had crunched into William's side of the car, and William had broken his neck instantly.

I was still the one driving. Who hadn't been able to get out of the way fast enough. I replayed it over and over again. I tried not to replay hearing the crack of William's neck beside me, the intake of breath before there was none. I just told myself they were nightmares designed to hurt me.

Nobody needed to know those existed.

"I still can't believe they took the business. They took everything."

I raised a brow. "They own the business. I was just working with Lauren."

"And William's sister is a bitch."

I didn't contradict her. My former sister-in-law *was* a bitch. A bitch that was mourning day in and day out, and needed someone to blame because she wasn't going to blame the fates, life, or God.

"I was a damn good pastry chef for them too. Our business did well. But she's doing just fine on her own."

Joni rolled her eyes. "Sure. As in they're not going bankrupt, but they've been through how many pastry chefs since? You were the best that they had, and they suck. I hope they go out of business. Or the place burns down. No one needs to get hurt, but let's burn down the place."

I shook my head, wondering how I got so lucky with my best friend. It seemed like these days I wasn't lucky in most things. "Thank you for the green bean casserole and the company. I'm going to get to icing. Do you want to stay and watch? Or do you have work to do?"

"Jeff's with the kids today for daddy-daughter outings, so I'm going to play on my phone for a little bit and watch you and keep you company. Is that okay with you?"

I smiled and nodded. "I would love that. I can always use the company."

What was left unsaid was that I rarely left the house anymore. I went to the grocery store, I ran errands, but I didn't go out. There had been that one disastrous date last year, when I told myself I would get out and try to see the world, which had ended with me crying in a corner, and the guy going back to his ex-wife.

Oh yes, I was a pro at dating. Considering I had never really done it and had married the first and only man I had ever loved. The one and only man I had ever been on a date with. The one and only man I had ever kissed.

So no, I was better off staying in my house, working in my house, and never leaving.

Part of me wondered if I should have just moved up north to my parents' town and started over there. It might've been easier all around, but I wanted to stay here. I loved it here. And there were plenty of clients who needed me here.

I was a hometown baker who didn't own her own shop because she lost the one she loved. Just like she seemed to lose everything.

And that was enough of that. My life kind of sucked, and I was in mourning still, but that didn't mean I was going to cry myself to sleep every night. Maybe tonight though. Tonight seemed like an okay day to do that.

I went to work, icing little high heel cookies and purses and fancy rings. It was a bachelorette party and the girls loved shopping and were doing an all-day shopping experience, complete with little cookies along the way.

I loved the designing, the filling, and icing. This order was pretty easy, not so delicate. I was grateful that today was only for a bachelorette party, and not the wedding cake I would be making in a few weeks.

No, I didn't need to think about that.

"Oh, that's terrible."

I looked up at Joni, piping bag in hand and frown on my face. "What's wrong?" My heart began to race, images of fiery car wrecks and people grieving beside graves filling my mind.

Joni winced and looked as if she wanted to talk about anything other than what she'd just brought up. "I'm sorry, it's nothing. Just a viral post."

"What kind of viral post?" I asked, setting the piping bag down and going to wash my hands.

"It's nothing."

I was slightly alarmed now because there was something wrong. There had to be, with the way Joni kept looking around the room as if something or *someone* was going to help her. "The more you say it's nothing, the more I feel like it is actually something. Come on, let me see."

"I shouldn't have said anything. I don't want to make you sad," Joni mumbled.

I held out my hand and she slid the phone towards me. My heart broke just a little at what I saw.

It was an Instagram photo of a beautiful wedding dress, champagne-colored, antique-looking. It looked as if it had been altered some but was still beautiful and timeless.

The caption beneath it broke my heart.

A Bride In Need.

Hi. I'm Augusta. I'm getting married in two days. No matter what, I'm getting married.

Only it seems that the world is making things a little hard for me. You see the dress in that photo? That was my great-grandmother's. And then my grandmother's. And then my mother's. Aunts have worn it, second aunts. I was supposed to wear it in two days. And because it needed to be altered, we went to a local seamstress. One who lied about who she was.

I gave over my dress full of memories, hope, and promise to a woman who pretended to be the former owner of a renowned business.

And then she closed up shop and took my dress, along with others. I'm never going to see my family heirloom again.

We will continue to work with the authorities to hopefully help find it for future generations of my family, and for our own sense of peace.

But I know I'm not going to be able to find it in two days.

I get married to the love of my life, to the man who has already moved mountains for me, in two days.

And I have nothing to wear.

Naysayers may laugh and say 'Wow it doesn't really matter. You are meeting the love of your life at the end of that aisle, it shouldn't matter what dress you wear, or what flowers are set, what music sends you to him. It should be about family.'

And in the end, it will be.

But my family dress is gone, and this day is about us. I just wanted to feel pretty for one day.

So I'm asking you a favor. Below are my measurements, something I never thought I'd post, but I am asking you for help.

Do you know where this dress is? Or do you have a way of helping me find a dress? I keep shopping, keep searching, but I'm not a size six. I'm not going to fit in a dress off the rack like some might be able to. I cannot find the dress that I want, or a dress that calls to me. I'm searching. I promise you. But I need help.

I'll keep searching, and I will wear a bathrobe to meet the love of my life if I have to.

But if you could help me find a way to be a princess, I will be forever grateful. If you find that dress, I will come to you. Or we will pay to ship it to us. But if you help me, we will be forever grateful. Please. Help me try to fix this.

I didn't realize I was wiping away tears until Joni handed me a tissue.

"Isn't that awful? I know today wasn't probably wasn't the best day for you to look at that, but it's just so terrible. I wish there was something I could do. My dress is collecting mothballs somewhere, and looks nothing like the one that she wore, and it wouldn't be the right size anyway."

I tapped my chin as I looked at the post from the Wilder Retreat and Winery.

"I know this place. It's on the other side of the city, but I've heard good things. Didn't Bethany Cole get married there?" I asked, speaking of the Oscar award-winning actress.

Joni snapped her fingers and nodded. "You're right. Same as Lark Thornbird. It's the up-and-coming place to get married. Although not only celebrities get married there, as is evidenced by this couple. I cannot believe that seamstress did that."

"People can do terrible things, and they don't think about those they hurt."

My heart ached, but I realized that there might be something I could do. Something so outlandish, so ridiculous.

"I'll be right back," I said as I went to the guest room, knowing this was probably a mistake.

It wasn't even going to work out anyway.

But I went to the closet and pulled out the large box

I had taken with me in the move but hadn't known what to do with.

I heard the gasp behind me but ignored Joni as I opened the box. It was a sense of mourning for me, one more nail in the proverbial coffin of my marriage.

I shuddered, hating that thought.

"It's beautiful, Aurora."

"Did you know I was named after a Disney princess?" I asked, my voice soft.

"Yes. And I know that you couldn't decide between a blue or pink gown for your bridesmaids."

"And so I mixed them, a nod to my fairytale movie."

"What are you thinking, Aurora?" Joni asked gently.

"I'm thinking that William's not coming back. That I re-steamed and got this dress ready for something."

"Aurora."

"Did they leave a contact number?"

"Are you sure it'll fit?"

"I think so. It's not exactly the same, but the lace is delicate enough, and mine has a longer train. Maybe they can make it work. I don't know. It would be nice for it to have a second life, don't you think?"

Joni handed me the phone and I looked up to see tears streaming down her face.

"I already entered the number, you only have to hit call."

"Okay. Here goes nothing."

The phone rang twice before a woman answered, sounding out of breath, slightly frazzled, and it settled my nerves. "Wilder Retreat and Winery, this is Alexis, how can I help you?"

I cleared my throat, knowing that tears would come if I let them. "Hello, I'm Aurora. I saw your Instagram post."

"So have a few others. We're so grateful for the response."

My heart ached a bit, but I kept going. "Have you found the dress or a replacement dress?"

Alexis answered. "We haven't, but we're still on the lookout. We keep getting calls wanting updates, I'm sorry we can't give you another one."

She sounded like she wanted to hang up, to move on to the next call or the countless other things this woman had to do, but I continued. "My husband died five years ago today," I blurted, not quite sure why I said that. Jodi's eyes widened, but then she made a continuation movement with her hands, and I realized that that probably wasn't the best place to start.

"I'm so sorry. I can't imagine that loss."

"I hope you never have to. Truly. But that was my awkward way of saying that I still have a wedding dress, and one that I think that will fit Augusta. I live about an hour away, on the other side of the city. But if you want, I don't know, I'd love to see if it would fit. I can head over right now with it. I don't know, it just feels right. If she would be okay with wearing a dress of a woman who lost her husband. But now that I think about it, that sounds weird."

I could hear the tears in the other woman's voice as she too cleared her throat. "I think that is the most giving thing I have ever heard in my life, and I would love to see the dress. Can you send a photo? That way I have something to show her while we wait. No matter what, we would love to have you here, Aurora. It just sounds like you need to be here too."

I swallowed hard, grateful that I wasn't crying even though Joni was.

I snapped the photo and texted it over and heard Alexis's gasp when it came through. I just sat there, holding the connection that I had with William, the memories it entailed.

But I knew I was doing the right thing.

I couldn't hold onto the past forever. Couldn't hold onto what wasn't there. But if I could help this person, maybe it would ease the pain.

It wouldn't make it worth it, nothing could.

But maybe I could make a difference for someone else.

CHAPTER THREE
RIDGE

My feet slammed into the ground as I jumped over the brick fence and ran after my quarry. The man panted as he ran, camera flapping and slapping against his back since he had tossed it around his neck as if that would keep it from strangling him. I rolled my eyes as I gained ground and caught the guy by the arm. The sleazy online magazine photographer tripped over his own foot and nearly faceplanted onto the limestone. I almost let him but wasn't in the mood for a lawsuit. These guys loved suing if they got hurt running away from our property after they trespassed. Fortunately for him, I kept him upright as he flailed and shouted about his rights.

I fisted my hand at my side. His eyes boggled as he looked at my fist, then up at my face.

"Really? Are you going to sue me for chasing you on our property when you're trespassing trying to get photos of what, the foliage?"

"I have every right to be here. I am a paying guest."

He slid out a room key, and I just shook my head. That room key had been lost last week. These guys never learned. He would've probably made more money by snapping a few photos of my famous family members by actually paying for a damn room. Instead, he used a key that some guy had probably found on the floor, or sold, so he could pretend he was allowed to be on site. Guests had to be screened and sign non-disclosure agreements. That was in the rules. If you wanted to stay here, or come to the winery, you had to be aware that if you sold photos of any famous people on the grounds, you would not be welcomed back. You could take pictures of course, we couldn't stop you, but if you sold them? We'd find out who you were and then you couldn't come back to visit. So making a quick buck on a photo of Lark sitting on East's lap at our new distillery as the two of them laughed really didn't seem worth it.

Because that twenty-something girl who had giggled the entire fucking trip might've made some money, but she wasn't allowed to come back. Even for her sister's wedding.

This guy was also trying to earn that quick dollar, but he did it for a living.

He was the worst of the fucking worst, and I was so tired of this part of my job. It was hard to keep people safe when they acted like fucking idiots.

"Please stop. Just shut up. I really can't stand your complaining."

"I'm here as a guest. I swear. I'm taking photos of the sunset."

"It's morning."

The hot wind of a Texas fall slid over us, and the man swallowed hard, eyes darting around as Trace came forward but didn't say anything. My boss just folded his massive arms over his even more massive chest and glared at the dumbass.

"As you were saying?" I asked, my voice deadpan.

"I have every right to be here. I wasn't taking photos of anyone."

"The thing is, you don't have every right to be here. And you're going to have to show us your camera. You saw the notice posted when you walked in. Even though you don't have a legal key and you don't have any right to be here."

I wasn't a hundred percent sure that was exactly correct, but the guy didn't seem to know any better. He just began crying in earnest, cursing us, and handed over his camera.

Trace looked through it, brow raised, but shook his head.

"Which one?"

"Both of them. Walking down the path on their way to help Kendall. You know, just living their lives. And you can't help but be a nosy asshole."

"You can't take that photo from me. That's my camera. I have rights."

I shook my head as Trace handed over the camera.

"You keep saying things about rights, but you really don't understand, do you?"

"I don't need to understand. I'm just taking photos. I can't help who's in them."

"You can go ahead and sell that. Make a couple dollars off two women who just happened to be walking down a fucking path. But I get to do my favorite thing." Trace gestured behind him, and the man looked like he was about to piss himself as two deputies walked forward, scowls on their faces.

"You see, we're not going to take your things, we're not going to beat you up. But you are trespassing."

"And this is your second strike here," Trace put in. "Isn't it, Ronnie?"

"Fuck you."

"No thanks. I'm good. But you enjoy your time explaining to these nice deputies why you're once again being a nuisance."

"He's all yours," I said, gesturing towards the scowling paparazzo.

"Okay, come on, let's talk about what it means to be a trespasser on private property," the deputy said as Trace just shook his head and followed along.

"You can head back over to the event. I've got this."

I nodded, called in the incident to the team over the mic, and headed back to the pre-wedding event.

At least there was some excitement for the day, though I was still a little annoyed that I'd had to run in my nice shoes.

Since we were working on a pre-wedding, I had to look nice and not wear work boots. I just hoped I wouldn't have to get them resoled again. Or buy new ones. I hated shopping.

"Hey, there you are."

I looked up as Wyatt came forward, a scowl on his face. It seemed like the Wilder scowl was something we all had in common. He fit right in. "What's up?" I asked my brother. He had his long, brown hair pulled back from his face in a little stubby ponytail. The man was constantly growing it out and then hacking it off. I didn't know what the point was, but I figured tomorrow he might shave his head, just because he could.

He didn't have the big bushy beard like most of us, and his bright eyes seemed on the verge of anger, which was unusual for him.

Unlike our cousins, our traumas and anger didn't come from a military past. In fact, none of the four of us had joined up. We had all taken different paths, putting some of us in danger, and one of us into stardom.

I was the eldest of our set of siblings, though I wasn't as old as Eli, the oldest of the other cousins. I fit right in the middle, and I didn't mind. It meant that I could still be the annoying big brother, but I also didn't have to make all the decisions. At least when it came to this company. That was pretty nice.

"Gabriel said he's coming to visit soon."

My brows rose at the mention of our youngest brother. "Last I heard, he was out on tour, making millions and taking over the world. Not as much as Lark though. Did you hear how many stadiums she sold out in that last tour?" I shook my head, still reeling over the fact that Lark Thornbird was now a Wilder. Between her and Bethany, it felt as if we had walked into this random Hollywood fairytale.

"He is still is on tour, but they have a two-month break. I figured Gabriel was going to either work on more music, get laid a few times around the world, or really anything but want to hang out with his big brothers. But he said he wants to see us."

I frowned, wondering what that could be about.

"He okay?" I asked.

"No clue. He sounded okay, but it's Gabriel. He uses his voice for a living. He could probably lie easily."

"Well, since the latest news article I saw about him called him the typical slutboy with the voice of an angel, I don't think him gallivanting around the world is good. Maybe he needs to be here."

"We're all here for a reason," Wyatt said, but I didn't ask. He didn't ask me why I needed to be here, and I didn't ask him. Brooks was the only one we knew the reason he needed to be here, but we still didn't talk about it. The other Wilders seemed to love talking about their feelings and explaining why they were the way they were. Maybe that wasn't always the case, but ever since they got married, they seemed happier and more willing to talk about shit. That wasn't us, and we were fine.

"When's he getting here?" I asked.

"Soon, or so he says. He'll probably be a couple of days late, knowing him. But he'll get here, then we'll make sure he's fed and watered and gets sleep. And then we'll put him to work."

I chuckled at that. "You going to put him behind the bar again?"

Wyatt shuddered. "Never again. And he's not touching my distillery, and I know that Elijah wants him nowhere near the winery."

"So, is he going with Brooks or me? I don't think I can have him work security, considering he comes with his own."

"True. Brooks will take him on. Hand him a hammer and hope he doesn't smash his thumb."

"Then he couldn't play guitar, and all the girls would weep."

"Guys too. Don't forget that. People of many genders love our baby brother."

"He's an asshole, annoying as fuck, but we love him too."

"That should be our family motto."

I laughed, shaking my head as Alexis walked over, looking slightly frazzled, but a little less than the past day or so. I didn't understand how someone could lose a wedding dress, let alone an entire business, but I knew Alexis would handle it. And if she needed me to run out and find something for her, search high and low for some dress thief, I'd do it. Alexis ruled this place with an iron fist, and I'd do anything she asked.

Not that I'd let anyone know that. I had my badass image to uphold.

"Hey, you two. I'm off to see the bride. But we have good news. Very good news."

"You find the dress?" I asked, curious.

Alexis winced, her expression crestfallen. "No. The authorities are still working on it. But we might've found a dress that would work."

"Well, that's good. There's like a thousand dresses out there, right? She was bound to find one."

Alexis scowled at Wyatt, who held up both hands. "I'm sorry. I'm sorry. I know nothing about weddings."

I ignored the twinge at that, because I had never been married, but I nearly had.

She'd had her dress.

I quickly pushed those thoughts from my mind. They didn't belong here.

"Well, I put a post on Facebook and Instagram and anywhere else I could, and it sort of went viral."

"You really need something else going viral for this place?" I asked, thinking about the potential security issues.

"Not that kind of viral. I mean, at least I don't think so. A couple of news organizations picked it up." Alexis blanched and shook her head. "I'm sorry. I talked to Trace about it."

"Add me to the emails, because if I'm going to have to deal with this, I'd like a heads up."

"I promise it's all good things. But seriously, I think we found the dress."

"So someone just messaged and said they had one?" I asked, incredulous.

When Alexis teared up, I cursed.

"What the hell did you do, Ridge?" Wyatt growled.

"It wasn't me."

"It was neither of you, it was the whole story behind it." She let out a breath. "We're not going to tell the news organizations this, not unless Aurora wants us to."

"Aurora?" I asked.

"The woman who is letting Augusta borrow the dress she wore when she married her late husband."

Alexis immediately began to wipe away tears even as her phone buzzed with countless notifications, because the woman was always working.

Wyatt whistled through his teeth as I just stared past her at a woman with long, dark hair.

This wasn't the bride.

She had part of her hair pulled up away from her face, but the rest fell in long waves over her shoulders. Her light gray eyes seemed to pierce under the sun, but I could see the sadness in them. I didn't want to see that. I didn't want to see any of it. She had soft features, a small pert little nose, lush lips, and curves that could kill a man.

I frowned, wondering why the hell I was even thinking that. I did not think about women that way. Ever. Not since, well, not since ever.

"Oh, there she is. Aurora, come meet the cousins."

Aurora put on a strong smile, but it didn't look real. I had a feeling she didn't want to be here anymore than I did.

"Hello," she said, her voice soft and hesitant. She was so unlike Heather. Heather had always been strong and firm and told everyone exactly what she wanted. That was why I fucking loved her.

Why the hell was I even thinking that? Heather wasn't here. She was gone. I didn't understand. What was wrong with me?

"Hello, it's nice to meet you." Wyatt held out his hand and Aurora took it, then her gaze turned to mine and it felt as if everything had changed.

Something was wrong with me. Something was very wrong with me.

I needed to walk away.

"I'm Wyatt, by the way. And this is Ridge. He's a growly asshole, just ignore him."

Alexis gave us both a look, but I just shrugged, not saying anything.

The bride walked up; I recognized her from the meeting before. She had tears in her eyes and practically ran towards Aurora, taking her hands.

I wanted to be anywhere but there. I did not want to watch these two women speak, nor did I want to be part of this.

"Aurora, thank you so much again. You have to stay tomorrow."

Aurora looked shaken and took a step back, running right into me. I put my hand on her shoulder to steady her then immediately dropped it when she stiffened at the touch.

Good, I didn't want to touch her either.

"Oh, I shouldn't be here. This is your wedding."

"I know. And I would've been able to find a dress or pants or jeans or even that bathrobe that I talked about. This wedding would still have happened, but you are making it much more special. And I know the memories that go with that dress. Or at least I can imagine them. But you should watch those memories turn into something new. If it's too hard for you, I'll understand and you can go. You don't have to stay here, and I will ship your dress back to you all clean and perfect. Or you can stay and be part of this, like you already are. I can't even imagine what you're going through, but I will forever be grateful to you. And you helped save the day. Your memories saved the day. So, please stay."

Jesus Christ. This woman was laying it on thick, but every single word sounded true. Aurora was saying goodbye to her husband. The one she had worn that dress for, and now she was letting someone else borrow it. Either this woman was in so much pain she was trying to run from it, or she had the biggest heart out there.

Maybe it was both, or maybe we were all just so fucking delusional.

I wouldn't want anything to do with it. But then again, I worked around weddings day in and day out, even though I told myself that I didn't even believe in this shit.

Yes, we were all delusional.

Alexis opened her mouth to speak, but Aurora beat her to it.

"I'll stay. But these are your memories, okay? This dress will be yours. It needs a new life. It needs a new chance. So take it, and I will stay to watch you say your I dos and vows to your new husband. This is about you. Not me."

Augusta squealed and Alexis walked them off,

standing between the two women doing what she did best—handling them so no one felt awkward.

Wyatt whistled through his teeth again. "Damn it. Talk about heavy. Should we talk to Brooks? That way he's prepared if he hears about this?"

I swallowed hard, wondering what the hell he was talking about, but then I remembered. Brooks was also a widower. But the world knew about that. He hadn't hid the fact that he had lost his wife.

Nobody knew I had lost someone who could have been mine.

"Yeah. That way it doesn't get awkward. It's going to suck though."

"Yeah, but we've got this. But that Aurora? Not only is she a damn good person, she's fucking hot."

I forced my lips up into a smile and nodded.

"You're right. But maybe don't sleep with the grieving widow on the day that she gives up her wedding dress, okay? Don't be that asshole."

Wyatt shook his head. "I don't need those kinds of complications."

"No, neither do I."

I did the best thing I could do and pushed all thoughts of Aurora, her wedding dress, and those sad eyes out of my mind. Or at least I tried.

CHAPTER FOUR
AURORA

I should not be here. I should be at home with my cookies and my own thoughts. I did better when I was at home. I remembered exactly who I was when I was at home.

I didn't have memories thrown in my face when I was there. Okay, that was a complete lie considering I was surrounded by those memories.

They didn't do it on purpose. It just happened, but I knew the truth.

I was here for a reason.

Because Augusta and Alexis asked.

"I really cannot tell you how grateful I am," Alexis said as she came into the small alcove where I had been staring off into the distance.

I smiled at the woman with dark hair, bright eyes,

and a beautiful smile. Her cheeks were slightly flushed, and she wore a lovely and flowing pantsuit. She also held her tablet and a side bag that probably held a million little things to help the wedding go smoothly.

My wedding planner had been on the ball, but Alexis seemed to be in a thousand places at once, and I really liked what she had done.

"Are you sure it's not awkward for me to be here?" I looked around the part of the building that I could see, my heart swelling. "I can leave if it's too awkward for them. I'm a stranger. I feel like I'm crashing the wedding."

Alexis shook her head and reached out, gripping my hand. I froze, still not used to touch. Joni was really the only person that hugged me these days. Her kids, too, and her husband would occasionally give me a one-arm awkward hug. He wasn't too emotional but was always there for me.

YouTube tutorials and reading whatever book I could find meant that I tried not to ask for help with too many household repairs. Joni's husband stepped in when I didn't know how to change the flapper on my toilet, or when the hinge on my cupboard broke, and no matter what I did, I couldn't figure it out until I realized that my hands just weren't big enough to do it myself.

That was always the annoying part. I was independent, learning how to do things on my own that William had always done with or for me. Just like I had always done things for him. The feeling of loss after losing him wasn't just about the fact that he wasn't here. It was the fact that I had lost my partner in everything. I had to do his job and mine. And I missed touch. I missed hugs. I missed everything else that came with the intimacy of a relationship.

"You are welcome here. We want you to be here. However, if it's too much for you, you don't need to stay. I know we might have pressured you into this." Alexis winced and pushed back her hair, even though it still looked perfect. "We really are excited you're here and you're doing this amazing thing for her. But if you need to leave, you can. I'll make sure Augusta knows. Because while this is about her, it is also about you. And we want you to feel good."

I nodded and looked past her out the window again, at the rolling hills, at the beautiful architecture of this retreat. It felt so welcoming.

The building we were in was the main building, which was broken up into two separate wings. One held the restaurant and lobby, where everything was dark glossy wood. There were bookshelves that had the classics on them that seemed to actually be read, as well as books that guests may have left behind. The other wing held floors of rooms as well as offices, and I had gone into one of them to hand over the dress.

The outside of the building was painted white with dark shutters, cobblestones, and large light stone pavers setting the way for the valet. There was a huge, gorgeous fountain in the center that looked to be original to the building. I remember seeing on the news that there had been damage in the huge run of tornadoes that had hit the area a couple of years ago, though they seemed to have rebuilt. It was classy and gorgeous and fit South Texas. There were a few old barns that had been spiffed up. I knew one was the dance hall, another a ceremony area. I was staying in one of the cabins on the north side, where I could see the sun rise over a small hill. I hadn't ventured into the winery on the east side, or the distillery and bar on the west side. I passed by the signature restaurant coming through the front gates on the south side, but I had never been there. It seemed a place to go for celebrations and anniversaries. And I was still only just now getting used to eating on my own.

The restaurant in here had been kind to me when I came alone with a book and ate amazing food while drinking Wilder wine. People hadn't looked on me with pity, they hadn't come up to me and wondered why I was sitting alone. It just felt natural. The food really had been stunning, although it surprised me that the pastry at the end had been a little dry. I hated being that person who judged, but with everything else being so amazing, it was odd that the dessert hadn't been. Or perhaps I was just disassociating. After all, everything else had been wonderful. Maybe I was just looking for something to dislike because I felt so out of place.

I realized I had been staring off into the distance for too long, so I cleared my throat and looked back at Alexis.

"I'll stay. It's beautiful here. You and your family have done such a wonderful job."

Alexis's shoulders relaxed in relief as her smile brightened. "It really is a family endeavor. My husband and his brothers opened it, and they put their blood, sweat, and tears into it. I can't believe it's been over five years since I came here."

My eyes widened. "Really?"

"Oh yes. That's a story for another day, but I love being a wedding planner here. We're raising our daughter here, and she plays in the backyard with all the children who visit." Alexis put her hand over her stomach and my eyes widened, reaffirming my suspicions from earlier. "And soon we'll raise another one here, along with their cousins. It's the Wilder way, after all."

I smiled a real smile for the first time since I arrived here. "Congratulations. I've only heard good things about this place. It's gorgeous, and I want to thank you for taking the time to talk to me even though I know you have to be doing a lot for this wedding."

Alexis tapped her earpiece. "My team's on it, but I will go see Augusta now. She's putting on the dress."

My stomach clutched, and I nodded. She had to have seen the tightening on my face. After all, I felt it. "Please make sure she enjoys the day. I'm just sorry that she had any stress at all. My dress brought me so many good memories, and I hope it can do the same for her."

Alexis reached out and squeezed my hand again. "You are brilliant. And we'll see you soon. You have the timeline?"

"I know where to sit. I'll just walk around here for a bit longer, take in the scenery. I don't venture out too often since I work from home."

"You know, I think if we hadn't built a house close to here, we'd never leave the grounds. And while it's beautiful, it is good to get out every once in a while." She winked as she said it, and I nodded before she walked away, her high heels clicking on the marble.

"Aurora?"

I turned and smiled at the innkeeper. If I remembered right, her name was Naomi, and she was just as gorgeous as every other woman I had seen here. She had short brown hair, a pointed nose, and kick-ass cheekbones. I was a little jealous of those cheekbones.

"Hello there."

"Is there anything I can get you? Champagne? Sparkling water? I want to make sure you're enjoying your stay."

I heard the concern in her voice, but it wasn't pity. She knew the story, just like most of the people who worked here. I was pretty sure I was going to end up being the center of attention, but I hoped that nobody mentioned it at the wedding. I would hate for anyone to mention why I was there. I wanted to be there for Augusta, to see my dress make new memories, and then go home.

Because nothing else I was doing at home was working. I wasn't happy, I rarely opened the blinds and worked my ass off for barely above a living wage because I had lost the one job that I loved.

I needed a way to start over, and perhaps this was the kick in the ass that I needed. That spark that would burn through me.

Because nothing else seemed to be working.

"I'm fine, thank you. I'm going to go for a little walk before I sit down for the ceremony."

"Please let us know if you need anything."

"Of course."

"Naomi," a terse voice shot out from the other side of the building, and Naomi's features tightened before she gave me a barely real smile.

"If you'll excuse me." She whirled on her heels and stomped towards the very built and bearded man on the other side of the room. "Are you kidding me, Amos? Do not shout at me like that."

"Oh, we're going to have a talk."

They grumbled at each other, and my eyes widened as they walked away, and I wondered exactly what that was about. Then again, it wasn't any of my business.

"Did you hear about her wedding dress?" an older woman asked another guest as they walked past.

"I did," the second woman replied.

"I wonder how they fixed that. I know that photo went viral, and I feel so bad for the bride. We've known the groom of course for years, and we love seeing how happy he is with Augusta, but I can't even imagine what I would have done if I had lost my wedding dress. There's just so much that goes into the choices and the memories with that. It's the one day it shines, and no matter what you do you'll look back on those photos and remember how you felt in that dress, and how you felt when you saw your groom while wearing it. And now she's going to be wearing what, something off the rack? Something that doesn't match what she wanted? Or maybe some secondhand thing that she found at Goodwill?" The woman shook her head. "I can't even imagine."

"What does matter is that she's marrying the love of her life. She could be dressed in a burlap sack and still be beautiful."

"True, I just hate the fact that the wedding dress is usually where you begin planning. And if you get married at a place like this, with that Alexis Wilder as your wedding planner? You know it was planned to a T. The flowers and the linens and the lighting and everything."

"I'm sure they'll figure it out. They handle celebrities and royalty. I'm pretty sure they can handle this."

"Oh yes, yes. But I still wonder what they did for a dress."

They kept moving towards the ceremony area, and I rolled my shoulders back.

I was going to ignore getting kicked in the pants today. I didn't have anyone to sit with, no one to talk to, but they wanted me here, and if this was the first step I was taking on getting out of my own way, I would figure it out.

Even if I had no idea what I was doing.

I made my way into the ceremony area as one of the

ushers gestured for me to sit on Augusta's side. I suppose I was on the bride's side.

I should just go. This was just a little too much. I missed William with every ounce of my being. I loved him. I always would, but it was different now. I could see myself as the person I was now without him. I wasn't the Aurora of my marriage. Nor was I the Aurora who had ground her way through the betrayal that death brought. I was now the Aurora who was alone, perhaps a little lonely, but resilient.

I just wasn't sure if I could watch that dress and have those memories play in my mind.

But it wasn't my dress now. It was Augusta's.

I knew I didn't want it back. She could have it and those memories. Today I would say goodbye.

Something caught my attention out of the corner of my eye, and I turned to see the man I met the day before, Ridge. He was on the security team, and a Wilder if I remembered correctly. And the way he had stared at me made my stomach clench.

Not in a scary way, or perhaps that was a lie. Because something scared me.

I hadn't felt that rush in so long that I had forgotten what it was.

Because that man, even with his harsh angles and growls, was beautiful. Those piercing eyes, that strong jaw. And those muscles? I hadn't thought of muscles like that in a very long time.

I was a single woman after all, which was a very weird thing to think. There was nothing holding me back. Except perhaps today of all days wasn't the time to think of it.

But when would the time be right?

He met my gaze and nodded but didn't smile. He just turned and went back to whatever his job was for the day, leaving me feeling slightly bereft.

What was wrong with me?

Music began to play, and I sat back in the bench as the ceremony began.

A little girl with a beautiful lacy pink dress skipped down the aisle, making everyone laugh as she tossed petals into the air and twirled like she was a ballerina. Then she set the basket down and proceeded to do somersaults to the end.

A smile broke on my face, pushing through any nerves, and I laughed along with the others, shaking my head as the harried mother came back to pick up her daughter, as well as the basket.

The little girl waved at everyone over her mom's shoulder, and I waved back, feeling lighter than I had in years.

The little boy was next with his ring pillow and was

very serious. Left together. Right together. Left together. Right together.

I hadn't even realized he was saying that aloud until people were laughing again, and I knew this wedding was going to be full of laughter.

The bridesmaids followed, meeting up with their escorts at the end as they helped them onto the stage. When the groom's eyes widened and a single tear fell down his cheek, I turned with the others, my breath catching.

There was Augusta, her eyes bright and wide and a smile so radiant on her face that she looked as if she were a goddess, coming to grace us with her presence and gift us with joy and love and happiness.

And her dress.

It was hers now. It wasn't mine. I still felt a kick in the gut that reminded me of the promise I had made to William. A promise we had kept but fate had broken. I would love William until my dying days, but as my dress became hers and she walked down the aisle, I knew that this was me saying goodbye to what was and what could have been.

It was time to make new promises, it was time to breathe again.

I let my tears freely fall as I watched a woman who, just days ago, had been consumed by panic and loss, marry the man of her dreams in a dress that reflected promises and memories.

And as they said their I do's, I wiped tears from my face and looked to the left again and met Ridge's gaze. He studied my face as everyone cheered and clapped. I nodded back, telling him that I was okay.

Because okay can mean a lot of things.

Today wasn't about me or my memories. Today was about the future.

And it was time to make that happen.

CHAPTER FIVE
RIDGE

"Let me deal with the drunk uncle, and then you're on five." I nodded at my team member and kept my gaze on the target.

No, it wasn't a target. I wasn't back in my old job. Thank God. Today was just making sure everybody got to their cars safely, didn't disrupt the wedding, and were generally behaving. They needed to eat cake when they were told, dance to random music that seemed to play at every event, and get party favors on their way out.

I still couldn't believe this was my job, but I liked it.

Trace and the others were covering the rest of the property. We had another team member at the inn, as well as numerous others throughout the winery and vineyard. Let alone the one working the wedding and out

Thankfully it was a slower day, and both Bethany and Lark had gone to New York for an award ceremony. I didn't know what award ceremony, nor did I know if they were nominated, performing, or just going to support someone else. All I knew was that their leaving the property didn't mean people stopped trying to take photos of them, and I had to escort a few photographers off the property. Then I'd had to make sure they stayed off, because some assumed that the girls would just circle back.

Because that's exactly what they wanted to do with their time.

I rolled my eyes at the thought and kept my attention on the task at hand, dealing with the drunk uncle. He was easy enough to get out of the way when his son came to collect him, so I called that a job well done. Knowing that, I still kept my eyes out for anyone who shouldn't be there, since not everyone knew the famous Wilder women weren't on property.

I liked Lark and Bethany. I liked Bethany's movies and Lark's music. But I had no idea why those two going into a restaurant needed to be national news. It was all over the internet, and apparently the two of them were constantly tagged by other people trying to speculate how the friendship was going now that they were married to twins. They fulfilled some form of fantasy for fan fiction writers out there.

But because they weren't on property, though their husbands were since they were working, it was a little quieter here. Not that I would say that out loud. If I did, something bad would happen. Because something always happened.

"Hey, is this the wedding with the borrowed dress?" a familiar and very welcome voice asked.

I turned to see my youngest brother, hat pulled down low over his eyes and a hoodie covering up his shape.

I hadn't known Gabriel was here yet, and if this was his best incognito look, it was no wonder he was plastered all over the news.

"How did you hear about that?" I asked, lifting my chin in hello as we made our way to the side. My replacement came to take my spot, so I was now officially off duty and could find out why Gabriel had decided to come out here now. He was the only one of us who hadn't moved to the small town outside of San Antonio. We all started over, while his life seemed to be exploding in some amazing ways. He had a few Grammys under his belt, and he was getting just as much press as Lark and Bethany. In fact, he had been linked to both of them in the past, although that had been invention by the media and fans.

Lark and Gabriel had done a song together at the beginning of their careers, and it won a Grammy and had been nominated for an Oscar for best song. And even though Lark was happily married, people still wanted the two of them to get together. When Gabriel had a small role on a TV show that Bethany had starred in, suddenly people decided that they needed to be together. I rolled my eyes at it, happy in my own relationship at the time. Then my life imploded and I kept it to myself, all the while not realizing that Gabriel was slowly sliding in on himself, giving in to demands that I couldn't even imagine. But he was here now, and that was all that mattered.

"The post went viral, man. Of course, I heard about it. And of course, it's this place that goes viral. You know, I realize that both Bethany and Lark want to come here to relax and not be in the spotlight, but you can't help it. Our cousins tend to make the news."

"So says you, the voice of an angel."

Gabriel scowled, and I held back a smile. My baby brother hated that title, something a famous magazine had said about him one year.

He had brushed it off, but people didn't really care what he thought. They wanted their perfect dreamy singer, so they were going to write whatever they wanted.

"Shut up. So, they found the dress? The only press that came out after the initial post was that they had found a dress, but all the details would remain with the family. I don't think Alexis was prepared for all of the press."

I agreed. "Hopefully it dies down. I met the lady that loaned the dress, and she doesn't seem like the type who wants to be in the public eye."

"That's good. So, it was actually a lady who let someone use her wedding dress? Not like a store who wanted to get some points in the media or something?"

"No. It is a woman who lost her husband and wanted the dress to do some good or something. Not quite sure, it's none of my business."

Gabriel winced. "I wasn't expecting something like that. It's got to be hard."

I agreed and wasn't sure how Aurora had done it. Then again, I'd never been married. Close, so fucking close, but never fully there. "Yeah. She's here though. Came to the wedding."

Gabriel looked over my shoulder as the bride and groom began to dance. "She's still there?"

"Stay away from her. You don't need to heal her wounds with your dick."

Gabriel winked at me as he mocked being hurt, sliding both hands over his heart, and staggering back. "How could you? How could you even think that? I'm an artist. And I want to protect her. For *art*."

"You're an asshole. And I don't know how long it's been since that woman lost her husband. So don't poach."

Gabriel scowled. "I'm not that big of an asshole."

"I know you're not." I paused, studying his face. "You doing all right, though? Want to talk about anything?"

Gabriel nodded. "Yep. I'm fine. Tired but good. Long tour. Have more to go. It's good to be near family though. You think Kendall will have food I can steal?"

He hadn't truly answered my question, but we Wilder brothers tended to keep to ourselves. "I'm sure there's something for you to eat. But Kendall is doing the work of two right now."

"Pastry chef being an asshole?"

"I love that you keep up with family news."

"I have to. All of you except Eliza moved out here, and Eliza's taking over the world up in Colorado, so I have to at least try to keep in touch."

"I guess you're doing an okay job with it."

"Gabriel?"

I cursed, annoyed at myself for not paying attention, even though it was my damn job. Gabriel was just as much of a celebrity as Bethany and Lark, and even though I wasn't on the clock anymore, I should still be alert. But then I realized who spoke and moved out of the way as Wyatt barreled into our youngest brother.

"Asshole. You didn't tell us you were coming in."

"I told you I was on my way. That should count."

Wyatt and Gabriel continued to wrestle a bit, and I just shook my head.

I cleared my throat and did my best big-brother voice. "Stop it, you two. We're in a place of business. At a reception. People just got married. Go wrestle somewhere else."

"Shouldn't you say he shouldn't beat up on the youngest brother?" Gabriel asked as he stood up, rubbing his shoulder. "How am I supposed to play guitar when I'm all bruised and bloody?"

"You did just fine when we were kids and you tried to jump from the roof."

"Excuse me, I didn't jump. I was pushed."

Wyatt rolled his eyes. "You tripped."

I held up my hands. "Not this again. I can't deal with this." My lips twitched though, as it was damn good to have the family together again.

"Come on, I'll make sure you get fed, and then you get to come work with me."

Gabriel gave Wyatt a dubious look. "We both know I don't work well behind a bar."

"No, but someone always needs to do dishes. Earn your keep, Wilder."

Gabriel had a put-upon look on his face, but his shoulders relaxed as Wyatt led him towards the main building to grab something from the kitchen. Something was going on with Gabe, but something was going on with Wyatt, Brooks, and me, too. Maybe we'd get to the bottom of it, maybe we wouldn't. But no matter what, we would all be together for a few days while Gabriel was here. And even though he was a multi-platinum-selling singer, with more awards than could fit in a single room, Gabriel was still the baby brother. And that baby brother needed us to take care of him.

The music changed and people started laughing as even more started to dance.

While I wasn't on duty, I still couldn't help but be on alert. You just never knew, and I needed to tell Trace that Gabriel was on property.

I shot off a quick text and Trace let me know that he was already aware, because the man apparently knew everything that went on at this property.

I was sliding my phone in my pocket when a familiar face caught my eye.

She was absolutely stunning with her hair flowing around her, a tiny braid intricately woven along the side of her head. She wore a long flowing dress that showcased her curves and made my heart stutter.

That wasn't something I was going to let myself think about, but damn it, she was fucking beautiful.

She seemed to sense me staring at her and looked up.

"Oh, it's good to see you again," she said as she pushed her hair from her face, her fingers twitching nervously.

I hadn't realized I had moved closer to her.

"Why am I making you nervous?" I asked, my voice low.

She swallowed, her tongue darting out to lick her lips. "I just don't really know why I'm here. Everyone's dancing and having fun and it looks like a blast, but it's a little overwhelming since I don't know anybody."

"I could see that being a problem. Nobody asked you to dance?" I asked, then realized that sounded like an asshole thing to say. "I'm surprised."

She smiled and relief spread through me. "I think they wanted to, but I sort of ran away. You know, the sane thing to do."

I shook my head. "If I asked you to dance right now, would you run away?" I hadn't meant for the words to slip out, I hadn't even realized I'd been thinking them at all. I should take them back. Walk away, pretend I hadn't. There was nothing of me left, not for this. But she would be gone in the morning. Who would it hurt if I just pretended?

She froze for a moment, then let out a breath. "I might."

"Good to know."

I was playing with fire.

When she looked up again, I was caught in her gaze. What was it about this woman that made me want to see who she was? "Anyway, they were going to do more speeches, and I really didn't want to be there in case they mentioned the dress." She winced. "Doesn't that make me sound like a fool. I came here and offered to let her have my dress, and now I don't want anyone to mention it. This day shouldn't be about me. I shouldn't have to worry that Alexis is afraid somebody might find out and it might go in the media." She put her hands over her face and let out the cutest little growl. I did my best to ignore it.

"We'll protect you from that."

She lowered her hands, frowning. "Really? You can protect me from what, people wanting to know why I would do such a thing? Or the fact that my former in-laws will probably use this as another reason to hate me, for daring to besmirch their memory of their precious son?" Her eyes widened, and she put her hand over her mouth. "Pretend I didn't say that. Please. There's no reason for me to have said that."

There was a lot to unpack there, but it wasn't any of my business.

"I'm a Wilder. And our family has some experience dealing with the media. I'm sure Alexis will do her best not to let your name out. And there's no way a news organization or anyone connected to them made it into this wedding. That was my job."

She relaxed marginally. "I forgot. Which is funny because it's sort of hard to forget the fact that *the* Bethany Cole and Lark Thornbird live here. And now that I think about it, Gabriel Wilder is what, your brother? Cousin? Long lost relative?" she asked, her eyes dancing with laughter. She looked so damn beautiful. I really needed to stop thinking that.

"Brother. So yeah, we can deal with the media windstorm. No one's going to bother you."

"I hope not. I also don't want to look at the bride. I mean she looks gorgeous, but that's her dress now. I don't want her gratitude to me anymore. It just reminds me, and I was finally okay. It's been five years. Five years, and I'm okay. It's just hard to remember that I'm okay when people want to remind me that I used to not be."

Her words hit home. Because she was right. It was hard to remain okay when others brought up when you weren't. Although my family didn't know what had happened, others had. That's why I had moved here. I had changed, I was better for it.

"Do you need me to get you out of here?" I asked.

She shook her head. "I just didn't want to be the center of attention, but I'm glad I did it. I feel relieved. Which I know sounds weird, but I do. I just, this was a good idea. A weird one, but a great one."

She was smiling then, full-on smiling, and I didn't even realize I was doing it until I was pushing the braid behind her ear.

She froze, her lips parting when she looked up at me, and I couldn't help but look down. And then I realized what the fuck I was doing, and she seemed to as well. We each took a step back, and I realized that I had nearly kissed a fucking stranger. She smiled brightly, and I knew it was fake, but I didn't mind it just then. I needed it.

After a moment, she finally spoke, breaking the moment we both desperately needed and yet couldn't have. "I'm going to...head back to my cabin. It's lit up and I can see it from here."

She gestured towards the cabin at the far end of the path, and I nodded. I didn't offer to walk her because I knew that would be a mistake. I wouldn't see this woman again, and I was grateful for it. I missed Heather, and our daughter or son, but I wasn't *in* love with Heather anymore. I had moved on over the past two and a half years, at least marginally. But there was something about this woman, something that told me that my version of moving on was a farce.

Because I hadn't been with anyone since Heather.

From what I could tell, this woman hadn't been with anyone since her husband.

We were just sparks turning to ember, and I needed this to fade away.

I cleared my throat, pulling myself out of my thoughts. "Nevertheless, I'll make sure one of our team members makes sure you get to your cabin safely. It's dark, you could trip."

"I'll be okay."

"I'm sure, but it's all part of the duty. And this way you can make sure that you really get out of this without somebody asking you to dance. Or wanting to thank you again."

Her gaze searched my face, and I cooled it, making sure she couldn't read what I was thinking.

She nodded, and I spoke over my earpiece to make

sure she had someone to escort her to her cabin. I watched her walk away without another word.

I had almost kissed her. Without even thinking, I had almost laid my lips on hers and broken my cardinal rule.

No more connections, no more grief.

No more complications.

And the woman who had just selflessly given her memories to another to make them smile was a complication.

CHAPTER SIX
AURORA

I zipped up my small suitcase and wondered when I would wake up from whatever dream I'd fallen into, like Alice's trip through the Looking Glass. It didn't seem real, and yet here I was, the day after a wedding that I hadn't planned on attending, for a couple I didn't know. A wedding that had fundamentally changed something deep within me. I wasn't the same person who had looked at the viral post. Nor was I the same person who had given Augusta my dress.

Because it wasn't mine anymore.

It was hers and that was truly all that mattered.

It was what I needed it to be so that I'd feel fine.

It was also the morning after a night in which I had the strangest dreams I'd had in years.

Dreams that hadn't been about my past, hadn't

been about cupcakes or cakes or imagination and creativity. They were all about a certain bearded man who I had nearly let kiss me the night before. It might've been a few years since I kissed anyone, more years than that since a *first* kiss. But I remembered the look, the feeling of your heart when it beats so loudly you could hear it.

It was so weird to me that after all this time, I could still *want* that. Then again it shouldn't. I was moving on. I'd been on dates. *Two*, but they counted. I tried. I was doing my best. And yet everything felt different now.

Should I have let him kiss me?

I didn't have an answer to that, but it made me wonder why the dreams were so vivid.

Maybe that wasn't it at all. Maybe I was just seeing things because I felt attraction for the first time in far too long. I didn't have answers, but at least I probably wouldn't have to see him again. He wouldn't be waiting for me outside my small cabin, nor was he going to walk me to my car, or check me out of the inn. In fact, I didn't even have to check out. Naomi, the innkeeper, said that all I had to do was check out on the app. I thought it was pretty amazing that the Wilders had their own app. That all of the individual businesses on the property were integrated. I even had a guest profile where I could look up my stay or book another one, or make reservations at the spa, for wine tours, dinner at the main restaurant, or even just for appetizers and small bar plates at the distillery. Getting into the signature restaurant was a little harder and required advance planning, but they did keep a few emergency tables open for last-minute additions.

I could book another stay if I wanted to, one where I wouldn't have overwhelming *memories* on my shoulders.

What an odd thought, but perhaps that's exactly what I needed.

I needed to make decisions to find my next phase of life. I couldn't continue to work in my kitchen. I had a small online business, and it was barely paying the bills. I hadn't touched William's life insurance, except to ensure his funeral had gone along with his wishes and to pay for his cremation.

Though his ashes weren't at my house.

His mother had them. I hadn't even felt too pained about that, other than the fact that she literally stole them. I'm sure a law or two had been broken, but I didn't care. Those ashes weren't *William.* I hadn't wanted them in my house, staring at me, knowing that I was going to move on. Or at least pretend to. I hadn't actually done that yet, but I needed to.

I needed to find a new way to work, a new way to make friends outside of Joni and her husband. I would do that. I would be strong. Except I felt like I was continually making mistakes and setting myself back because I didn't want to say goodbye.

I looked around the small gray cabin with its warm and inviting touches, and farmhouse chic aesthetic. A place like this was meant to welcome you and be a place you could call home for a few days. Maybe I would do this again. Maybe I would spend some of that money I saved for a trip with William and come back and figure out exactly what I wanted.

I needed to step out of the shadow of my in-laws, step out of the shadows of memories that carved notches into my heart with each passing breath.

And I would.

Giving away the wedding dress had been the first step. A step I hadn't even realized I was taking until I picked up the phone.

The only reason Joni and her family weren't here was because I wanted to do this alone. To prove that I could. That they were the only people I could rely on locally told me I needed to make changes.

I needed to make a choice. To move on. To grow up. To prove I was fine. Because I was.

I didn't feel the devastation within me with every passing breath like I used to.

Perhaps that was growth. Perhaps that was betrayal. Or perhaps that was living when the world around you fell apart. I didn't have answers, but I would need them soon.

So, while I could use the app to check out without saying goodbye, I wanted to see the place one more time to decide if I should come back.

Today was a day of new decisions.

I rolled my suitcase out of the cabin and thought again of the night before. Of the near kiss that never was. He hadn't walked me to my cabin, and for that I was grateful. I knew he had his own reasons to stay away, and it wasn't my place to ask why.

But he still kept me safe. And while that was his job, it felt different, good.

I made my way down the path, nodding and smiling at a few of the guests who were out for a walk or to enjoy the scenery. It was quite gorgeous here, and a part of me wished I had more time to go to the spa and the winery. I told myself I would come back. I was ready to make changes. Doing something for myself seemed like a good change.

One of the staff members smiled at me as they opened the door to the inn.

"Thank you."

"No problem. I hope you had a wonderful stay."

I smiled, surprised by my answer. "I did. Thank you so much."

"No problem. Hope to see you back soon." They moved on, talking into their headset, and I wondered what they did. They might be security, or work on the grounds. I wasn't sure, but there were so many moving parts of this establishment, that I knew that whoever was in charge had to have spreadsheets upon spreadsheets in order to keep it running.

"Hello, Aurora." I looked up to see Naomi smiling at me from behind her large desk, tablet in one hand, a notebook in the other.

"Good morning. Am I interrupting?"

The innkeeper shook her head. "Oh no. I'm just doing my morning walkabout and list-making before I get set for checkout and check-in. It's going to be a beautiful day, and I'm sad to see you go. Was everything to your liking?"

"It was honestly so beautiful." I looked around the large entryway, the comfortable seating, books and plants everywhere. It felt like a home and also a high-end getaway. "This place is absolutely gorgeous."

"I love it. I'm so blessed to be working with the

Wilders after all these years." There was something in the other woman's voice, but I wasn't going to pry. I was still curious about the man I had seen with her before though.

"They're lucky to have you. You're so nice."

"I try. That's a big part of my job."

"You do quite well from what I can see."

"Well, thank you. And honestly, it was a pleasure to meet you. You did such a wonderful thing, and there aren't any words for it."

My heart swelling and still feeling awkward, I lowered my head and shrugged. "I don't mind. It was lovely to see everything, and to know that I could help." I cleared my throat. "I didn't want to check out through the app because I wanted to have a reason to come back in here, but is there anything you need from me to check out?"

"Oh, no. You're fine. And even though you gave me your credit card before, you will not be charged for this trip. This one is on us."

My eyes widened. "Oh no. This place is so beautiful. You're not going to be able to keep it open if you give away nights."

"It was two nights, and the Wilders want to make sure you know that they are so grateful. The bride and groom also tried to pay for your stay, but we wouldn't let them." Naomi winked. "You saved us. It's the least we could do."

Embarrassed, I wrung my hands in front of me. "I wasn't expecting that. I was fully prepared to pay." And dig into my savings since I was running on a very tight budget with my current awkward jobs.

"You don't have to worry," Alexis said as she walked into the entryway. "I was going to mention it, and then we got distracted with the dress and everything. Seriously, it's on us."

"Well, I'm just really glad I could help. The wedding was beautiful. You guys do such a fantastic job here. No wonder you have a waitlist."

Alexis beamed. "Well, the Wilder men had a good thing going, and then the Wilder women showed up and made it even better." She winked, then startled as a curse exploded from behind her, and a gorgeous woman with dark hair piled up on the top of her head and flour all over her chef coat stomped in.

"He's gone. The asshole's gone." The woman froze and blushed when she saw me. "I didn't realize anyone was in here. I'm so sorry. Please ignore this and know that the Wilders are happy to have you here."

"Kendall," Alexis said, her voice exasperated, yet there was worry on her face.

I wasn't sure what to do, but I couldn't just stand

there awkwardly. "It's okay. You look like you're having an emergency. It's really okay."

Kendall, who I remembered now was the head chef for the inn restaurant and Signature, put her hand over her face and groaned. "I'm so sorry. Yes, I have a temper, but I don't usually throw myself into awkward situations like this. At least not since the twins were born."

Alexis cleared her throat. "Please don't tell me your pastry chef quit."

"Oh, he did. And he took the designs. The whole *book* of designs. I have a backup, but my notes were in there for the wedding tonight! And tomorrow. I'm going to go commit murder." Kendall turned to me. "Please don't let anyone know that I admitted to that, or if the authorities question you after I do, go ahead and tell them. They'll still have to find the body."

Naomi paled as Alexis pulled out her phone and began tapping away. "We'll get the lawyers on that. I mean the stolen book, not murder. We don't condone murder. I'll talk to Trace. There's no way he could just leave without letting you know. Especially with the security on our property."

"Oh he did. The asshole didn't want to work, and now I'm screwed. I don't have time to finish the cake for tonight, or make the cake for tomorrow, let alone all of the desserts, chocolates, and other favors. I can't handle it. I can't believe I just said that. I never say things like that."

"Babe? What's wrong?" a very handsome man who looked somewhat like Ridge said as he hugged her from behind.

Kendall seethed. "I'll tell you what's wrong, our pastry chef just left because apparently he couldn't handle a woman telling him what to do."

The man pinched the bridge of his nose, an angry flush rising in his cheeks. "Okay, who do I have to kill?"

Kendall smiled, even as tears of rage filled her eyes. "I love how we both went straight to murder. But there are witnesses now, and I guess murder's not the way to go. I don't know how I'm going to be able to do it though. With Sandy gone, I just can't do it all."

"I'd offer to help, but I accidentally burned that pot when I was trying to boil water for eggs."

"We don't talk about that," she mumbled.

"I could help," I blurted, not even realizing I was going to say the words until they were already out.

"I'm sorry, what?" Kendall asked, her voice sharp, but not unkind.

Then Alexis snapped her fingers, as if remembering something I was probably going to regret. "Yes, you can. I've seen your social media and your website." She turned to Kendall. "This is Aurora, the dress fairy from yesterday. She's also a pastry chef and used to have her own bakery and everything."

"I used to work *in* one," I corrected and then flushed. "Well, it was my in-laws' bakery, and when my husband died, well, let's just say I couldn't work there anymore. Not that I usually tell anyone that, but considering I've just offered to help you, maybe you need to know my references?" I asked, my voice going high-pitched at the end.

Kendall looked at me. "You used to work for Francis a few years ago, right?" she asked, tilting her head as if she could pry my entire baking history out of my brain. I had a feeling she could if she tried hard enough.

I blinked. "How on earth did you know that?" I asked, confused. Francis was a high-end cake decorator in downtown San Antonio that did weddings with the rich and famous of South Texas. Whenever a celebrity wanted to get married down here, or a country music star visited and wanted to have a party, he was the one they went to. He retired right before William died, and moved to England to be with his wife. His second in command had taken over the business, promptly running it into the ground. I moved on to the bakery with my in-laws at that point, since I had thought I was family. So many wrong decisions, and yet, here I was, offering my help.

"I remember you. Francis was a friend for a while. Do you still have it in you? Because you were a brilliant cake decorator, and I remember your pastries."

I nodded and blushed. "I own a small online shop where I cook from my house now. Not so glamorous, but I can step in. I mean...if you don't mind. At least until you figure out what to do."

"Oh, you're so going to regret saying that, because I remember your cakes. You're with me. Let's make sure you still have it." Kendall reached out and grabbed me as Alexis beamed.

"I'll get the paperwork ready, or at least make Eli do it. And thank you once again for stepping in, Aurora. I'm so glad you called because we desperately needed you."

Kendall pulled me away and I nodded in thanks, my breath coming out in pants.

They needed me.

The Wilders needed me.

And I was going to show them that their trust in me wasn't misplaced.

I was a damn good baker. A fantastic cake decorator. I could make mille-feuille like nobody's business and ice cookies as if I was born for it. And despite what my former in-laws said, I was damn good at my job.

Kendall practically pushed me into the kitchen and I went through her notebook, trying to help her remember the notes she had taken for the client.

I knew this was change.

It wouldn't be permanent; it was just for a day or two, until they could figure out what to do.

But this was still a change.

And the exhilaration running through my veins reminded me that change could be good.

Change could be thrilling.

Now it was my time to feel needed. Finally.

CHAPTER SEVEN
AURORA

I wasn't sure how to summarize the last four days. I had a brand-new job at the Wilder Retreat & Winery as the pastry chef and the wedding cake lead. I got to make wedding cakes and desserts for a living again, only on a much grander scale because they had at least three weddings a week. I didn't know how this had become my life, but I loved it. I was a baker, and I loved my job. I was no longer stuck in my house, baking cookies and small orders, and hoping that what I did was enough. Because it was never enough.

"Okay, Aurora. You're coming to the 1:00 p.m. meeting, and then the 3:00 p.m. meeting. We have the Torkland bride and groom, and then the Ashton bride, and the Merriment bride right after."

I grabbed my tablet and quick notes, as well as

looked through the wedding book Trace and Ridge had somehow gotten back from the former pastry chef. I wasn't sure I wanted to know how exactly they had retrieved it from him. I only knew that the police weren't called. Somebody made a rumble or two, but no blood was shed, and Kendall hadn't had to murder anybody. I also had the lovely joy of fixing every little thing my predecessor had done. It wasn't that he was a bad baker—it was actually the exact opposite. He was good at what he did, he just didn't like dealing with happy ever afters. He hated weddings and hated listening to Kendall. So no matter what the Wilders did, they would never be good enough for him. And he was an employee. Just like I was now an employee. I almost needed to pinch myself to make sure this was real, but it was. I was now working full-time, with benefits, and already having an amazing time.

Yesterday was my first appointment with Alexis to meet a bride and groom and go through their initial meeting to find out exactly how they wanted their wedding. I had sat back and only asked a few questions at the end while Alexis handled the rest. Honestly, I wasn't even sure she needed me there. But one of my favorite parts about being a baker for weddings was getting to know the bride and groom. That way I could customize their cake and any desserts they wanted specifically for them. And since I didn't have to do this full-time, because there was enough kitchen staff to ensure I wasn't the only one baking day in and day out, I also was working on desserts for the inn's restaurant, small dessert favors for weddings, and if Signature needed me to step in, I would. They had a dessert chef on staff there in their own right. However, if there was a large party, I could be there to help.

I was working far more hours for far better pay than I ever thought possible, and I loved it. Yes, the commute sucked, but in terms of city driving, it could have been worse. And it was one straight highway thanks to the Loop, so I only had to deal with the construction from hell and the overpass that was never going to be completed connecting downtown San Antonio to downtown Austin. That was never actually going to happen, and we all knew it. But we could pretend it would be complete sometime in the next twenty years of construction.

"I've got it on my list. Anything else?"

"Not from me," Alexis said as Kendall frowned at her phone.

"No, we're good. There're a few other things that we have to handle throughout the week, and I know you still have a few other projects from your previous job."

I nodded. "I had already said yes to a few clients,

and I'm grateful to be able to use your kitchen to get them done, especially since you didn't have to allow that."

Kendall waved it off. "You stepped in at the last minute and are completely changing your life to suit my needs. I'm just happy that fate decided to put you in my path. And yes, I sound very selfish right now, but after the issues we've had since Sandy left to pursue her dreams, I feel like I'm thirty steps behind and deserve this. I deserve you."

I smiled while shaking my head. "You're ridiculous and I love working with you."

"We're going to have to put that on my business card." Kendall winked and Alexis shook her head.

"Okay, a few more things to go through and then I'll let you get to work. I know between your sous chef and the staff at Signature, you have everything covered but, Kendall, you're going to need to hire another chef. Signature is becoming a thing, and I know you like working there, so we're going to need someone to take your position here."

Kendall frowned, and I almost felt like I should leave; this was probably a conversation they had often. Honestly, I wasn't sure how Kendall had done it at all. Between the inn's restaurant, catering events, and working at a high-end restaurant that was only open a few hours for dinner, Kendall had to be working far too many hours. Plus, she was a mother to twins, and from what I heard, she and her husband were trying for another. There weren't that many hours in the day.

"I know, I know. I'll find someone. But now I don't have to find a pastry chef that can work the weddings. And Jeff is great at Signature," she said, naming the pastry chef who worked there. "But he cannot decorate a cake to save his life. He doesn't like doing it, and he doesn't like weddings. Just like the guy we don't talk about that used to work for me here. You have to actually like weddings and love in order to do it, and neither of them understood that."

I swallowed and shrugged. "I believe in all of that. I love weddings, although I'm glad that I don't have to stay for the whole thing." I hadn't meant to say that last part, and both women gave me a soft look but not a pitying one.

"Either way, hire someone. I'm the one saying it."

"I know we keep going through people because they want their own restaurants and they don't want to work for me. And because I work them hard."

"I'm going to step in and put my foot in my mouth here and say if you're working them too hard, and you're also doing their job, then they are not working hard enough and you're working far too much."

Kendall gave me a look while Alexis just laughed.

"I knew I loved her. Now, go forth and make people happy and bake and cook and do all the good things with food. *And* look at that stack of resumes. It's time."

Kendall grumbled but headed to the kitchen. I looked over at Alexis. "I hope she doesn't hate me. I mean, I really like this job. Though I wasn't expecting it."

"Wasn't expecting the job, or wasn't expecting to like it?" she asked, a teasing light in her eyes.

I stood up, tablet in hand. "Maybe both?"

At the exasperated look on Alexis's face, I smiled. "I honestly never thought I'd want to go to a wedding again in my life, and not only did I go to one, I ended up with a job where I get to work at them. I used to make wedding cakes and birthday cakes and cupcakes and cookies and breads and all these other things when I was at the bakery, but it wasn't weddings day in and day out. It was all kinds of celebrations. And I know I can do a little of that here, because it's not just weddings, like tomorrow I'm making a retirement ceremony cake, it's a little different. It's throwing myself into the deep end and remembering that it's okay."

"You are so freaking resilient and amazing. I am so happy you're here, but if it is a little too much, please let us know. We will find a way to make it work. We're really glad you're here. And one day soon we're going to sit you down with some wine and cheese in the employee section of the winery, and you're going to spill about why you're not working at your other place anymore."

My shoulders stiffened and I forced myself to relax. "There's not really a story there."

"You can lie to yourself, but that lie isn't going to work with us. When you're comfortable, just know that we Wilder women sort of collect people."

At my raised brow, she continued. "You work for us now, and you don't have to be our friend—because there needs to be a healthy divide between work and real life sometimes—but if you'd like more friends, we'd love for you to join us. I promise we're not a cult."

That made me snort, and we made our way towards where we each worked. "Isn't that like the first thing a cult says?"

"Maybe. But we have wine and cheese, and you can bring the dessert." She winked as she said it, and we said our goodbyes before I headed into the kitchen. Today, I was working on a small two-tiered wedding cake, and then a groom's cake. We had meetings later, and then I would do the finishing touches on the prep for the retirement cake. Dessert tonight for the restaurant was simple—mostly pies and cakes and tarts. I worked on those each morning, so by the time lunch and dinner rolled around, they were all ready to go. Signature didn't need my help for the next week, but it would be nice to brush-up on my high-end skills when they did need it.

No day was going to be the same and every cake was going to be different and fit the personalities of those involved. Every tart and pastry and cupcake would be a new experience.

Joni had always told me I needed to go out and find something new. To remember that I was still here even though William wasn't. I hadn't let myself before. Maybe it was time I finally listened to my best friend.

And as if I thought her into existence, my phone buzzed and I looked down at the text.

Joni: *Kick ass today. Bring home leftovers. We miss you.*

My lips twitched as I texted back.

Me: *I can probably do that, at least with the leftovers. I'm still new enough that I'm slowly working my way up to kicking ass.*

Joni: *I'm sure you're already doing it. I love you and I'm so proud of you. And I can't wait to visit you because that retreat has always been on my bucket list.*

Me: *I'd love to see you here. Now I have to get to work. My boss hasn't seen me text yet.*

Joni: *Ooh, already in trouble.*

We said our goodbyes, added heart emojis, and then I washed my hands and got to work.

Kendall was working on prep for the restaurant now, and would head over to Signature later, which was the job that she really loved. I wasn't sure how she did it, and I knew that if the Wilders had their way, there would be a new head chef for the retreat and for catering. Kendall was doing the job of three people, and that was honestly ridiculous. From the way that her husband glowered at her after a long day and would pick her up and carry her over his shoulder back to the car to take her home, I knew that he was frustrated too. But their relationship dynamic was adorable and, if I did say so myself, the Wilders were damn sexy.

It was a little distracting.

I put my earbuds in and got to work, rolling out the fondant for my fall-themed cake. It was a lemon cake with buttercream frosting and strawberry and rose filling. A little high on the flavor points, but it was their favorite flavors, and chosen by my predecessor. I wasn't going to change anything, other than elevate the decorations as much as possible. The sketch that he left had been bare bones and the only reason I even knew where I was going was thanks to the additional notes Kendall had found. Now, I'd be working on making it spring on the inside and falling leaves on the outside. Considering we rarely had seasons, I liked that this cake seemed to want to have both. I'd be doing fondant leaves changing from green to the oranges and browns and yellows of autumn and working with food coloring for most of the afternoon. It was sometimes monotonous work, but fun. I enjoyed this part, even though my predecessor hadn't.

I had already worked on the desserts for the restaurant and some pastries, and tomorrow morning after I did my initial restaurant set, I would work on the chocolate bowls and other specialty chocolates for the favors. I would get it done, and I was grateful that this was my job now, instead of sitting at home and wondering when my life would begin again.

"Aurora?"

I turned to Naomi, noting the hesitation in her voice. "Yes?"

"There's someone out front for you, and they said it was urgent. I'm sorry for interrupting. I know you're busy."

Alarm spread through me as I quickly set everything down and nodded to one of the kitchen hands to take care of my station. I washed my hands and followed Naomi out.

"Did they say who it was?"

"No, just that it was urgent, and you needed to come out there."

Visions of Joni not being able to reach me and something being wrong with the kids filled my mind, and I pulled out my phone. I had no missed texts or calls, but maybe she was out of her mind and unable to communicate that way. Maybe she needed to tell me in person.

"They were...insistent."

At the oddness of Naomi's tone, I knew exactly who was out there and I rolled my shoulders back, sliding my phone into my pocket.

Because Joni was fine.

Instead, Lauren stood in the center of the lobby, face pinched, hair piled on the top of her head. She had on suit pants and a white button-up shirt. She must have just come from an event—she was a baker as well and worked smaller weddings in the city. I remembered years ago, right before everything changed, she had said she tried to work here, before Kendall and whoever else had been in my job before me had been hired. I'd always found that odd since they had a family-run bakery, but she had talked down about Kendall and the rest of the Wilders, saying they weren't good enough.

But that was Lauren. Anything that wasn't hers, that she couldn't have, must not be good enough.

"Thank you, Naomi. I'll handle this."

My voice had been low so Lauren hadn't noticed me yet. Naomi looked back and forth between us.

"If you need help, just let us know."

I nodded and stepped forward, clearing my throat. "Lauren? Is everything okay?"

I shouldn't have asked that. Because things weren't okay. She hated me and her brother was gone. What was I supposed to do? I couldn't change the past. I couldn't bring him back.

"Well, I see things haven't changed. Keeping me waiting."

I barely resisted the urge to roll my eyes. I was better than that. I didn't need to act as immature as she was.

"I'm working, Lauren. Is there something you need?"

"I need you to get your head out of the clouds and get back to where you belong."

I blinked, confused. "Where exactly do I belong? I'm working here."

"With our rivals? William would be ashamed of you."

It was like a slap and a gut-punch at the same time, and I staggered back. Just a single step, but Lauren saw it, and that catlike smile jumped to her face for an instant before she narrowed her gaze. My former sister-in-law had already won, and I needed to get out of this before we made a scene and I lost the job that she hated so much for me.

"You're being ridiculous, and you need to leave. I'm working. There's nothing I can do for you, and honestly there's nothing you need from me."

"How could you? How could you betray my brother's memory like that?"

"For doing what I do best?"

"What you do best is ruin everything. This place keeps stealing our business, stealing William's family's business, and you decide to work here?"

Her voice rose, and I saw Naomi on the phone out of the corner of my eye. I resisted the urge to close my eyes and sigh. Well, there went this job. I knew I couldn't have anything good when it came to this or my life. Because something was always taking it away.

"You need to go. You're grasping at straws here, and remember, you're the one who kicked me out of the business. I have no loyalty to the bakery. Only to myself. You made sure of that. And we both know that the bakery and this establishment barely have any connections. Your business is strong, the Wilders won't change that."

"Is there a problem here?" a deep voice asked, and I closed my eyes, humiliation settling in.

Ridge stepped to my side. Not in front of me to protect me, not behind me, but at my side. I would have to think about what that meant later. He folded his arms over his massive chest, but I didn't look at him beyond that. I sighed and looked at my former sister-in-law. For some reason, Lauren looked between us and scoffed.

"Calling security on me. Really?"

"No, that was me," Naomi said, giving a little finger wave. "We protect our team here."

"She's just going to fail and make things worse. That's what she always does."

"Ma'am," Ridge began, but I held up my hand.

"I'll handle this. Thank you, though," I added quickly, meeting his gaze. He searched mine for a moment before he nodded and let me speak.

I would be grateful for that later. For now, I couldn't think through the humiliation. "Lauren. Go. I don't know what you're trying to do, or what you want from me. But you're not going to accomplish anything. I haven't worked for you for five years. I have taken scraps since then, but I'm done. You're embarrassing yourself and you're embarrassing me. This is a place of business. People come here to be happy and relax. You shouldn't be here."

"We'll just see about that," she grumbled before she stomped off, but I knew that wouldn't be the last of it.

Lauren didn't hate me for not working with her, because she had been the one to fire me in the first place. Lauren hated me because I was alive and her baby brother was dead. I had lived, and William hadn't. Lauren would never forgive me for that.

"Are you okay?" Ridge asked and I stiffened, hating that he had witnessed that scene.

I turned to him, and once again there was that flare of attraction. That burn in the belly that told me I wanted more.

Who was this man, and why did I feel like this?

I ignored the tension, the way that the hair on the back of my neck rose. I could reach out and cup his cheek, just touch him.

And maybe that was part of the new me, starting out and branching out.

But right now it was too soon, at least because I really only knew his name.

"Thank you. I'm fine. If it happens again, I'll escort her out."

"If it happens again, I'll do it myself," Ridge said, his

voice low, deep, and it did horrible things to me...things I needed to ignore.

Today was a day for new beginnings. And maybe this beginning was just my job, just doing something I wanted.

Or maybe it was about that heat, that connection, because Ridge hadn't moved his gaze from me, and I didn't want to move my gaze from him.

And then I heard someone talking, a phone buzzed, a clock chimed, and real life entered. I cleared my throat and turned, heading back to work, but I could feel Ridge's eyes on my ass the entire time.

So maybe there was room for growth.

Or maybe I was just kidding myself.

CHAPTER EIGHT
RIDGE

My phone buzzed, and I looked down at the readout before hitting ignore. There was no reason for me to answer that call. Honestly, there was no reason even to send them to voicemail. They would know I ignored the call, and they would leave another ranting voicemail, just like the others. I would delete it like always because I didn't want to hear their voices. They bothered me every once in a while and would continue to do so until our dying days, because they could, and no matter what I did, they'd keep doing it. I also didn't want to fill up my mailbox when I needed to save space, because it was the only way I could hear her voice.

The sun had begun to set over the hills as I stood on

the property, the day settling on my shoulders and my shift over.

I hadn't expected to like living here. I had just needed a change when I went to my cousin Elliot and asked for a job. I needed a new place. Then I had gone to Trace and offered my services. Trace needed help with the security of the retreat, and I was damn good at my job.

It meant that I had to answer to others, but because my brothers and I had bought the property attached to the retreat, we were all in it. We all had our names on the deed and were part of this.

Even if it felt odd, as if this were only temporary. But it didn't feel as temporary as it had before. How could it when we had put down roots? A literal foundation, in Wyatt's case. He built an entire bar and distillery on the property. We had used the template from my cousins' friend Roy, but we were making our own Texas-based vodka and selling it locally. With the way Wyatt planned, there would likely be Wilder Vodka and more in grocery stores around the country. I wasn't quite sure we'd make it that far, but we'd try.

My cousin Eliza's family was distantly connected to a whiskey distillery, and so Collins Whiskey from a town up in Pennsylvania had sent over one of the brothers and helped us set up. Between our family and

Eliza's, it seemed we had enough connections that we could pretty much build anything we wanted. Hence the winery, distillery, and so much more. We were a full multimillion-dollar operation, and it felt weird that it was my job to keep it safe.

Though sometimes it felt as if I wasn't keeping my people safe.

I nodded at some guests who walked by, drinks in hand, on their way to one of the evening events. It was a retirement party of some sort, complete with a cake that looked damn delicious. I had tasted a few of Aurora's goods, and I was glad that she had been hired. I was a man who liked cake. I liked baked goods. But the fact that it was Aurora making them? That might be a problem because I couldn't stop thinking about her.

I looked at my phone again and pressed play on a recording that I had heard countless times.

"Hey, babe, just got back from the doctor, we have a new photo of the baby! I'll see you soon. I know the parade tonight is going to be long and tedious, especially with two high school bands competing. But it's a tradition and I'm so glad that you're going to be there. I love you."

I listened to it one more time, but the familiar sense of heartache and loss wasn't as strong. That was Heather's voice. I hadn't been able to make it to that sonogram, though I had been there for the first one. I had been called in for an emergency where I had nearly come to blows with the owner of the building we were trying to protect.

I had missed the second sonogram of our child, but I had held the picture in my hand that afternoon.

It fell out of my hand at the first sound of gunshots. The screams confirmed that something was wrong and when the car had barreled towards us, I had dropped the photo of our child so I could try to protect Heather.

And it hadn't been enough.

I had lost everything that day, and I was just now figuring out if I had anything left.

I didn't know what was going to happen next, how long I would stay here, how long I would need to, but coming here was the best thing I could have done. Even if that meant I had to ignore phone calls. There was nothing they could say that I hadn't already told myself.

"Ridge?"

I turned, my shoulders stiffening at the sound of her voice.

Aurora was wearing dove gray pants, comfortable shoes that looked like Crocs or like some form of clog. They weren't the sexiest shoe ever, but she bounced in them. She had on this three-quarter-length white shirt over a gray tank top, and somehow that made her look younger and more carefree than I had ever seen her. In the days since she started working for the Wilders, she had brightened up. Even after her former sister-in-law had made a scene.

The only reason I had even stayed back and hadn't said anything to that woman was because Aurora had asked me not to. And I hadn't minded, because seeing Aurora stand up for herself had done something to me.

I knew she had pain from her past, but I hadn't realized we had so much in common beyond loss.

We had the travesty and anger of others at our sides when we hadn't asked for it.

I had wanted to ask her why. Why her sister-in-law hated her and what happened. But it wasn't my place.

I needed to get away from her—because I wanted her.

And that was a problem. I wanted Aurora. Maybe it shouldn't be a problem. We were both adults, as free as we were allowed to be with our pasts winding their spindly fingers around our necks.

"Aurora. How was the kitchen today?"

She put her hands on her hips, the action pushing her chest out so I could see more of her cleavage. I made sure my gaze was on her face and not anywhere below her neck. I couldn't be that asshole. I shouldn't want her.

I was afraid I wasn't going to be able to do that either.

"It was good. I saw you sneak a piece of that chocolate cake."

My face went expressionless. "I have no idea what you're talking about. I can neither confirm nor deny I was anywhere near that cake."

She smirked. "I hear things. You might be the eyes of the operation, the all-seeing security specialist, but I know my cake."

"It had fudge frosting. It was damn good cake."

"Wasn't it? Recently the cakes I have been doing were all planned by my predecessor, but soon the desserts will be all me. I love this job. Everything is so different. I get to work on a variety of little things that culminate into this amazing moment for someone. They're making memories and I'm making cake and I love it." She shook her head, laughing softly. "And I am apparently in need of something to eat I guess, because here I am, rambling about baked goods when you're probably out here either working or needing some space. I'm sorry, Ridge. I just really love my job. And I didn't think I was ever going to get that satisfaction again."

"So, you had a good day then," I said, a smile crawling across my face. "I did too. Didn't have to break up a single fistfight or break a camera. No paparazzi, no drama, just a damn good day. And I had some fantastic cake."

Her smile brightened her face, and I wanted to keep that smile on her face for as long as possible.

I wasn't sure if I was the guy for that job, but part of me wanted to be.

"It really was damn good cake. And a great day. I was going to go get some of that cold fried chicken and potato salad that Kendall left for me. Do you want to join me? Unless you have other plans. I just don't want to head home yet, because the traffic right now is going to be a nightmare."

I frowned. "How far is the drive?"

"An hour, hour and a half with traffic. I can get it down to forty minutes though if I wait about an hour to leave. So I'm going to eat dinner here, and then head out."

I shook my head. "That's too far of a drive."

"Not in Texas terms. It's okay. My car gets good gas mileage, and if I have to stay too late because of a brioche or a design that's going to take forever, I can stay in one of the cabins or at the inn. It's not ideal, but this is worth it. Honestly, this is so much better than working out of my own kitchen at home."

She bounced in those clogs of hers, and I shook my

head. "We need to find a way to make that work better for you."

"Yes well, with the housing market as it is, I'm going to be keeping my tiny little house for a while. There's no way I can afford anything else right now. But anyway, I'm going to go get something to eat. You don't have to join if you don't want to, but I thought I'd offer. Mostly because my stomach is growling so loud, I'm pretty sure you can hear it."

I had been able to, but I shrugged. "Kendall makes some really good fried chicken."

"And it's cold, which is the best fried chicken unless it's directly out of the fryer. There's just something about cold fried chicken outside on a blanket with the breeze in your hair after a hot Texas day."

"I don't know, have you ever had cold fried chicken on a beach?"

"I haven't. Doesn't sand get everywhere?"

We headed towards the employees' area of the kitchen, walking side by side, our hands nearly brushing.

"Sand can be an issue, but if you eat it quick enough, it isn't. And isn't that protein or something?"

She threw her head back as she laughed, looking gorgeous as ever, and I swallowed hard, wondering what the hell was wrong with me.

Nobody was in the kitchen when we went in, and we grabbed a couple of sparkling waters, potato salad, fried chicken, and a small veggie tray that Aurora put together in no time.

"I figured I should probably eat my vegetables. You know, minerals and all."

"And maybe vitamins too."

I had no idea what I was doing, or why she'd even offered, but I wanted to. I'd deal with the consequences later.

On our way out, I picked up one of the outdoor blankets that were beside the door for guests and gestured towards the hill in front of us.

"Pick a seat, and let's eat some dinner."

"This place is beautiful. I hate the phrase 'things happen for a reason,' but maybe some things really do happen for a reason. Or maybe I'm finally living in the moment."

I shook out the blanket, and then we were piling the food on top of it, both of us keeping far enough apart that we weren't touching but could still eat in relative peace.

We were out of the way of any prying eyes from the inn and any of my family members. As soon as I sat down, I realized this felt like a date, and we weren't date people. Were we?

No, this was just food while we waited for traffic to die down so she could go home. But I didn't need any questions from my siblings. Especially when I wasn't sure I had any answers to give.

"Okay, I have no idea what she puts in the breading, but I'm going to go beg her to make some more."

"We can take turns begging. Because oh my God, I love it." She smacked her lips together, and I grinned, shaking my head. "You know what would be good with this?"

"Chocolate cake," we said at the same time, and she giggled.

"I ate too much cake today when I was prepping, plus I had two tastings today, and both of the clients wanted me to eat with them."

"And I had two slices of cake earlier."

Her eyes widened. "Two?"

"See? I see all and know all. Because you only know about the one piece."

"Diabolical."

Her voice trailed off as she watched the sun set. The fairy lights and walkway lanterns started lighting up so the place was still safe enough to walk around, but not bright enough to ruin the stars.

"I wanted to thank you, for before."

I looked over at her. "For what?"

She met my gaze, a wry smile covering her face. "Don't act coy. For yesterday. For backing me up when I needed it, and for being there when I needed the help. You somehow found the perfect balance of support and letting me handle it, and I didn't even have to say a word."

I shrugged, looking down at the blanket between us. "I'm curious though. Why didn't you just punch her and tell her to leave you the fuck alone?"

Aurora let out a small laugh but sobered quickly. "Because that wouldn't do anything. I'm trying to start over. Putting my fist in my former sister-in-law's face wouldn't help."

I raised a brow. "It might help a little."

"I met William when we were in high school," she began, and I froze, knowing that she needed to tell the story, but I wasn't sure I was ready to hear it. We had both experienced loss, but she didn't know my story.

No one did.

"You don't have to tell me if you don't want to," I whispered.

"No, I don't mind. After this many years I don't mind. It actually helps to tell the story, you know." She looked away, as if she were seeing into the past, and maybe that's what we both needed. "We met in high school. Sort of fell in love, but mostly just bonded over teenage anger and angst. We eventually fell in real love. Got married, and I joined the family business. William was an accountant and a businessman. He ran the bakery, and three other businesses that his family owned. He and his father were really good at that. They had just finished opening up a car dealership as well. I worked with my mother-in-law and sister-in-law at the bakery. I was a cake decorator and did the small intricate details because I was best at it. Something that my sister-in-law Lauren hated."

"She sounds like a peach."

"She was always a little jealous of the fact that I was a little bit better than her at some things. But she was happily married and a mom and had her own life. And then William and I were in a car accident. A drunk driver went across the road and hit us. I was driving."

I hadn't even realized I had reached out to grip her hand until she looked down at where I touched her, but I didn't let go.

"I was hurt, I broke my arm, which meant cake decorating was going to take some time to get back to. I was bruised and had a lacerated spleen. But William died. I lived and he died. It took me a few years to be able to breathe when I said that."

"What about your family?"

"They came down to help. I wouldn't have been

able to do anything without my mother. My parents have lives and jobs up north, but they put everything on hold and came down to make sure I was safe. They wanted to take me home with them, but for some reason I thought that staying here and not upending my life when my life was already upended would be helpful. I thought I had a job here and that my in-laws needed me. But that wasn't the case."

"What happened?" I asked gently.

"When I was finally ready to go in and bake with one hand, and had enough energy to stand for hours even though I felt like I was dead inside, my sister-in-law took me aside and said that she couldn't fire me but I wasn't welcome there anymore. She couldn't look at me anymore. I remember her speech word-for-word, and I still hate her for it even though I only feel pity now."

"What did she say?" An uneasy feeling filled my gut.

"She said that every time she sees me, she's reminded that she's mourning. That her brother wasn't there. That he spent his last years with me and not with them. He was theirs first. And she couldn't look at me and not see her baby brother. The little boy who laughed when she played with him. And he was gone and I was there, and she couldn't hate me but wanted to."

Anger slammed into me, a familiar ache that made me want to lash out and shake those people for daring to hurt her. But it wasn't my place. "How fucking selfish."

"Yeah. It was. I had to start over from my house. Start over with everything. I had to move because I needed a new start, but I didn't move far. My best friend and her family were there, and William was still there. At least the memories. I needed some of them, just not all of them. So, that's my story and why my in-laws suck. And this is a new beginning for me. I feel like it's a new beginning. I needed this. I didn't realize how much I needed it."

The sadness was gone from her gaze, replaced by a purpose, a light and a joy that I hadn't seen in her before.

And even though she had just told me of her sadness, of her pain, it was that joy that brought me in. I leaned forward and cupped her face.

She paused and looked up at me before nodding ever so slightly, giving permission before I could even ask. I brushed my lips against hers, once, twice, and then deeper. My tongue darted out and tangled with hers as she moaned into me.

She tasted of our dinner, of cake, of Aurora. She tasted of sweetness.

When I pulled away and pressed my forehead to hers, we were both breathing heavily, just a kiss, with so much wound around it.

"Well."

She looked up at me and tilted her head.

"Well."

She sat back and drank a big gulp of her water. I did the same, wondering if I had made a mistake.

"So, what's your cake for tomorrow?" I asked, changing the subject. She gave me a grateful look, and then we talked cake.

And nothing else. At least for now.

CHAPTER NINE

AURORA

I suppose I should have felt guilty, for the kiss, for an accidental dinner that might have been a date —or perhaps it was just dinner. But I had no guilt, no shame.

I could be completely kidding myself, but what was the point?

What was the point of that guilt when I felt like I was doing something right for once? Maybe I was doing something for me.

My stomach tightened at the memory of his lips on mine. I could still feel his fingertips on my chin as he angled my mouth and deepened the kiss. He had been in control. The push and pull between us and it felt lovely. Odd that it could be so thrilling yet gentle. It was everything that I could have wanted and more.

"Are you okay over there?"

I nearly fumbled the piping bag in my hand and forced myself to get back to what I was working on, the lovely spring fling cake for an upcoming bridal shower, and not whatever had happened the day before with a certain Wilder.

What was it about these Wilder men? And why did they make me feel like things could change for the better?

"Sorry, daydreaming while I'm supposed to be working on something intricate. I think I need more coffee."

Kendall gave me a look that said she didn't quite believe me, but how was I supposed to say that I had kissed her cousin-in-law and wanted to do it again?

That was a revelation—I wanted more.

I had been living in my own shadow, my own darkness and grief, for so long that it didn't yet feel real that I was allowed to have more. But I was. Because he was *more*.

There was probably something wrong with that and I would have to think about it in excess later. But for now, everything was *more*.

"You seem happy. I'd like to think it's all from the new job and working with me, but I don't know. I think it might be *someone* instead of something." Kendall sing-songed the last part of that sentence and I shook my head, a smile playing on my face as I went back to work.

The spring fling cake was a vegetable cake with cream cheese frosting and fruit and fondant flowers decorating the entire thing. All they told me was that they wanted something that was different, not the normal chocolate or lemon or vanilla, and when I suggested a vegetable, they were all for it. This had been a last-minute addition to the menu, which was why the time between the meeting and making this cake happen was so short, but I was enjoying this, and I was a huge fan of zucchini cakes. They were just as sweet, just as filling, and the cream cheese and fresh fruit were what made it stand out.

"That looks delectable. I'm very happy that you made an additional sheet cake on the side so we could all taste it. I haven't had a good vegetable cake like that in forever, and I'm a carrot cake fan."

"I actually like zucchini and other squash cakes more than carrots. I think it's because you don't add the raisins and shreds of carrots in it. Either way, though, it's all about the cream cheese frosting," I teased.

"You're right about that. I'm going to force my kids to try a bite." Kendall winced. "Not that your baking requires force."

"But it is still a vegetable and not just sugar. I understand." I smiled, thinking about Kendall's kids, because Reece and Cassie were the cutest. That morning, they had been in there "helping" Kendall with kitchen prep. Meaning they had been in the office playing with pots and pans and asking when they were allowed to cook.

"Thank you again for showing the kids how to decorate cookies. I've shown them before, but I think they like strangers more than me right now. Because I'm Mom and make them do their homework."

"I cannot believe you're a mom to twins."

"Tell me about it. Evan and I feel older every day, but I don't mind it. They keep me young and make me feel old at the same time. I think there's some time paradox when it comes to kids."

"That's what I hear."

Kendall met my gaze, opened her mouth to say something, but must've thought better of it and shook her head and went back to work.

"Most people just come out and ask."

"That would be an asshole thing for me to do," Kendall put in, raising a brow. "We were talking about my kids, so the first thing that came to mind to ask was about you. And then I realized that was an idiotic subject. Because no matter what I say, it's me putting my foot in my mouth."

I shook my head, that familiar ache hitting me, but it wasn't quite as intense. I was growing. Healing. That grief wave would hit again, but maybe it wouldn't be as hard as the time before. Maybe it'd be a little bit easier.

"William and I had talked about having kids. We just wanted to get the businesses set up first, plus we were actually enjoying traveling and each other. If kids came, we would've rolled with those punches, but we weren't actively trying."

"I'm sorry for bringing it up. You don't have to talk about it if you don't want to."

I shook my head, going back to work as I spoke. "I don't mind. Really. It actually helps to talk about it. Which is weird."

"No, I understand."

"Anyway, after the funeral, like minutes after the funeral, people would come up and say they were so happy and relieved William and I hadn't had kids. I was in a cast, barely able to walk, and leaning against my family members, and they told me they were grateful I hadn't had kids so I wouldn't have to deal with that excess burden. That those kids wouldn't have a father."

"Those fucking assholes."

"Oh yes. Completely. And then there were others

who said it was so sad that my life was wasted and my childbearing years were gone."

"Please tell me it wasn't those exact words? Because I have sharp knives."

I smiled even as that familiar anger hit. "Nearly those exact words. They were either upset that I didn't have William's progeny out there to grace the world or upset for me now that my one purpose as a woman in this world was beyond reach. Some even said I should get married right away because my ovaries had a ticking clock on them. You know, being in my twenties at the time."

"Seriously, who do I stab?" Kendall had a sharp knife in each hand. I shook my head, feeling exceptionally grateful that I'd found this place. Or perhaps it had found me.

"My best friend Joni pushed one woman nearly into a fountain before that woman's husband caught her. Joni swore it was an accident, but we all know it wasn't."

"I like this friend of yours. I can't wait to meet her."

"Oh, she can't wait to meet you guys either. She's heard great things about this place, and not just from me."

"We strive to excel." Her phone buzzed and she looked down at it. "And those are the kids. I should go meet Evan, and then I have a few other things to do. Have you taken your lunch break yet?"

I looked down at my phone and shook my head. "Time got away from me. I have a couple more flowers I want to set, and then I'll take my break. We have a long night ahead of us with this shower, and then the wedding."

"That's what we're here for. See you in an hour?"

"We both know I never take an hour."

"Do not tell me that. I don't want to know these things. Seriously, take your hour."

I waved as Kendall left, and I did my final settings before I chilled everything, cleaned up after myself, and headed to go get something to eat. There was an employee area where I could pick up the sandwich I had brought, or I could buy food at a steep discount from the restaurant. I was still on a budget, so I was trying to bring my lunch. Plus, I had eaten from the kitchen the night before, on the not-a-date dinner.

As if I had conjured him from my mere thoughts, Ridge turned the corner and I smiled at him.

Now that awkwardness settled in. I didn't know what I should be doing. Had that kiss been a one-off? Was he going to pretend it never happened? We were working though, so it made sense that maybe he wouldn't even acknowledge me. What the hell was wrong with me? Why was I acting like this?

"Aurora, you on your lunch break?"

He said a few words to Trace, who smiled at me before he got on the phone and walked the opposite direction. Somehow I found myself in the corridor of offices, standing alone with Ridge, at a loss of what to do with my hands.

"Yes, I was on my way to go get something to eat."

"I was doing the same. I was going to eat in my office, since there's a few outdoor activities going on today and I'm nearly peopled out after an incident. Do you want to join me?"

"Oh, okay," I said, nearly blurting the words. "What incident?"

"Teenagers, spray paint, and a dare. I'll go into details over lunch. But let's just say I think the parents were worse."

"That's usually the case from what I've seen."

We headed toward the lounge, since it was off the normal time for lunch, and picked up our bags from the fridge.

"I'm eating leftovers from two days ago. I was going to eat this last night, but then, well, I had a better offer."

Blushing, I shook my head and lifted up my sad little lunch bag. "It's a peanut butter and jelly sandwich. I bake for a living, but I get tired of cooking for myself."

"I can barely cook for myself. I mean, there's the obligatory steak and potato and a bag of salad, and there're a few other things that I've learned, but my brothers are better at it."

"I love cooking, but it's hard to cook for one. I'm not trying to get pity. I was just stating a fact."

He gestured for me to walk into the office before him and closed the door after he came in. And then we were alone, and my stomach was on edge. I knew it must have just been habit for him, but there was something different in the air.

"We're just having a conversation, Aurora, I don't pity you."

"Good. Because I really don't think I could stand that."

"Okay."

He had a little seating area in the corner of his office —a small loveseat and a tiny chair with a table between. I took the couch, while he stuffed himself in the chair. He looked uncomfortable.

"We can switch seats?"

"No, it's okay. This is a little higher than that couch.

I always feel like my knees are to my chin when I sit there."

"I take it you didn't pick the furniture?"

"No, this came with the building. There's a barn with the rest of the furniture that they rotate in and out so they don't get dusty or damaged from leaving things in storage for a while. I didn't choose this. I don't mind it, though I rarely use it."

"Well, thanks for taking the chair."

He winced. "You're welcome."

We talked about our days as we ate our lunches, and it felt nice. Like he was a friend. Maybe that kiss wasn't going to happen again, and maybe nothing more would happen except for friendship, but I liked the idea of friendship with him. I wanted it.

And I was grateful for these moments. Even if it felt as if I was standing on a precipice. Waiting.

We cleaned up our things after we finished eating and I stood up, but Ridge reached out and gripped my hand.

"Is something wrong?" I asked, my pulse racing.

"I was waiting to kiss you again. Are you still off the clock?"

His words slammed into me, and my tongue darted out to lick my lips. His gaze followed the action.

"I have another half hour."

"I'm pretty sure I can do something with that half hour." And then his mouth was on mine, and we weren't speaking anymore. We probably should have talked about this, should have gone over what exactly this meant and put a label on it, and yet why? Why couldn't I just live in the fucking moment? These moments were for him and for me and for us. So I dropped my container and wrapped my arms around his neck. The table was between us, and somehow he tugged me so we were at the side of the table, hands roaming all over each other. He was so much taller than me that I had to go on my tiptoes. When he deepened the kiss, lowering himself over me and bending me back, I groaned.

"So fucking beautiful," he muttered against my lips, and I breathed a sigh of relief as he kissed me again before trailing kisses down my jaw, my neck, and over my shoulder. He tugged my shirt aside, biting gently down on my skin.

"Ridge."

"That's it. It's just me. Just you."

With those words, I let everything else fall away. I needed this and even though it was probably a mistake, I didn't care.

Suddenly my back was against the desk, and he

nudged the computer to the side, somehow not knocking everything off the desk.

"I need to touch you. I need to taste you."

I nodded as he pulled off my shoes, then my pants.

When I tugged on his shirt, he grinned at me and slid it over his head.

"Tell me when to stop," he said softly, but I couldn't listen. It was all I could do not to swallow my own tongue.

This man was pure perfection. He had a few scars on his body, but he was all muscle. Firm chest, an eight-pack that went for days. He had a happy trail of hair that went down from his belly button, below the line of his pants, and I swallowed.

"How the hell are you this perfect?"

He laughed, shaking his head. "I have to be fit for the job."

"Just know that I eat what I bake. I'm all curves."

His hands were squeezing my thighs.

"That's exactly what I like to hear."

And then he was on his knees, and I was lost. He shoved my panties to the side, and I blushed in embarrassment but didn't say anything. I shivered as he blew cool air over my pussy before he licked, one long lick, then a second. Then he was devouring me, tasting me like I was his pleasure instead of the other way around.

I didn't understand how this could happen so quickly, and I didn't care.

I just needed this moment.

This was just Ridge and me. This connection. This was me living.

When his tongue hit *that* spot, I came, stars bursting behind my eyes as I nearly fell off the desk.

When he stood up and crushed his mouth to mine, I could taste the sweetness of myself on him. I should have been embarrassed, should have wondered why I was doing this with someone who was practically a stranger, but he wasn't a stranger. We had talked about things, we had eaten together, had hung out. We had seen each other every day for weeks. This, this was everything.

I was allowed to have this. No rules, no promises, just him.

"Aurora. Tell me when to stop."

I reached between us, cupping him over his jeans. He was hard, so hard and wide.

I swallowed. "Please, don't stop. But are you going to fit?" I asked, truly serious.

He grinned, catlike and beautiful. "Oh, we'll make it fit." He reached in his pants pocket and pulled out a condom. "Let's just say I was hoping. Please don't think I'm an asshole for that."

I took the condom from him.

"I'm grateful that you're prepared. And that you were even thinking of me to be prepared."

"Ever since I first saw you, I've been rubbing myself to images of you. You can call me an asshole for that."

I swallowed hard and shook my head. "I can't."

He leaned in and started kissing me again while taking himself out of his jeans. I gulped at the size of him, long and thick and wide. I truly didn't know if he was going to be able to fit, and I didn't care. It had been a long damn time, and I wanted him. Needed him. I slid the condom over him, squeezing at the base of his shaft.

"Be gentle, or this isn't going to take very long," he ground out, his voice guttural.

I nodded, then spread my legs wider as he positioned himself at my entrance.

I looked down between us. I needed to see this, I couldn't see the emotions—or lack thereof—on his face. I just needed this moment. And so did he.

The sight of him entering me nearly sent me over the edge; it was so raw and needy and primal and everything that I hadn't known I wanted. My body was too tight for him, and I was stretched almost to the point of pain. But then he slid his thumb over my clit, keeping me wet and right at the edge as he slowly rocked in and out of me. And then he was seated deep inside of me, and my legs were around his waist, and I was shaking.

"Ridge."

"I've got you, Aurora, I've got you." He slid his hands around my hips, holding my ass so I stayed steady on the desk. I nodded against his neck, kissed the skin there, licked and sucked, and then he started moving.

It was hard and fast and tight and wet, and it was everything.

When I finally looked up to meet his gaze and saw the way his eyes darkened at me, I knew this was what I needed. What we both needed. And then his mouth was on mine and I was coming, clamping around his cock.

"Aurora." He breathed out the word, sounding as if he was in pain, and then he was coming, his body shaking.

It felt like hours, but when we had both fallen, breathing in heavy pants, we held onto each other as the realization of what just happened hit.

I had just had sex with Ridge Wilder in his office. And I had no regrets.

This was the new Aurora. This was the Aurora I wanted to be.

I was afraid to look in his eyes, to see regret there, but then he pinched my chin and forced me to look at him.

"You're beautiful."

I swallowed hard, smiling softly. "I'm not ashamed," I said, an odd thing to say when he was still deep inside me.

He leaned down and kissed me.

"I'm not either."

"I can't be ashamed. Not when we both wanted this." I needed to make that clear. Because I couldn't feel pity from him. I didn't want it.

"I don't want to hurt you, Aurora."

Instead of hurt, instead of ache, I smiled. "So, let's not hurt each other."

He kissed me again and slowly slid out of me. He nodded, and I smiled.

We didn't talk about what this meant, what would happen, but we were not going to hurt each other.

And maybe that was the one promise we could make.

The one promise I hoped we could keep.

CHAPTER TEN

RIDGE

Water slid down my back as I pressed my forehead to the cool tile, trying to wake up after a long night of dreams, dreams that hadn't let me go.

I could not believe Aurora and I had had sex in my office. There had been no discussion, just need. Perhaps that's what we both needed. That hadn't been the first time we kissed, nor had it been the first time we looked at one another and seemed as if maybe we wanted more. And yet, it had been so different from anything I would have thought possible from the sweet and honest and innocent Aurora.

I thought perhaps I might have forced the situation, but she had been willing.

I couldn't believe what just happened, nor was I sure what I was supposed to do next.

After we had righted our clothes and I kissed her again, we went right back to work. There were weddings and parties to prepare for, and I had to keep the place safe.

And yet, how was I supposed to do that when my mind was on her?

The way she tasted, the way she felt. The way I had no idea what we were going to do when we saw each other next.

What the hell was wrong with me? Why couldn't two people just have sex and be with each other without all this thinking and this wanting and this guilt? Maybe it was because she was the first person I slept with after losing Heather. And I think I was the first person she had slept with after losing her husband.

It was just two people having survived loss coming together. In whatever way we needed. I couldn't say we were two widows, because I wasn't even a widower. Losing your girlfriend and unborn child didn't give you a label. It just left you with nothing. I still wasn't sure what I was supposed to call myself. But I moved away from the place where people still remembered me. Remembered us. Who knew what I lost.

I didn't know what I was going to say to Aurora

when I saw her next. I'd have to come up with something. I didn't want it to be awkward. We were two consenting adults who had held on to each other. She was further along in processing her grief than I was. Everybody seemed to know hers, while I still hid mine. Maybe that was a problem. Something I would deal with. But for now, I was going to get out of the shower, get to work, and see Aurora again.

I didn't want to talk about my feelings or anything like that, but there was an odd sense in my gut that told me that something was changing here. That this was important. I wasn't the kind of man who hurt women. So, I wasn't going to hurt Aurora. Only, I didn't want to get hurt in the process either.

That would be on me. I knew that. But did she?

I finished showering and headed to the kitchen to get some coffee and get ready for my day.

All I wanted was to figure out what the fuck I was supposed to do next and get through my day. It wasn't going to be easy, not when I couldn't keep my mind off Aurora, but I'd get through it.

It wasn't like I had another fucking option.

Once my travel cup was filled with coffee, I quickly made up a bagel with cream cheese and headed towards the rest of the day.

It was a beautiful morning, for which I was grateful.

It had been dark and gloomy the past couple of days, and I had a feeling that some of the recent weddings probably weren't happy with the lack of light for photos, though a light overcast light is generally nice for photos due to fewer shadows.

I smiled at myself, wondering why that had been the first thing that came to mind when I thought about the weather—the weddings, and this place of business.

I was damn lucky to do what I do. Not everyone was as fortunate to have a career that they loved, got to work with family, and mostly set their own hours. I worked with Trace, but if there were certain projects I'd rather work on, I had the option to. I owned part of the business, after all, even though I tried not to think about that. My life seemed so different than what I'd planned. Much like everything else.

There was a cool breeze coming in, and I was happy to be wearing my long charcoal-gray Henley and jeans, rather than a short sleeve shirt like I usually did.

People were milling about, coffees in hand, as they laughed with one another. Some families were out, kids laughing and screaming and running around, and I ignored the punch in the gut at that, because I wasn't going to think about *them*. They ran off to see the baby goats and chickens, which a staff member took care of so I didn't have to be anywhere nearby. I was all for trying to be sustainable, but I didn't like to deal with animals.

"Why are you up so early?"

I turned to see Gabriel walking towards me, Wyatt at his side. Wyatt had dark circles under his eyes and looked as if he hadn't slept much, while Gabriel, in all his rockstar glory, looked well put together, if a little unkempt with messy hair.

"You guys are up early, too, so why are you asking me?" I asked.

Wyatt rolled his eyes. "Slutboy over here wanted pancakes."

"Stop calling me slutboy," Gabriel muttered, his cheeks reddening as he looked around to see if anyone was listening. Thankfully it didn't seem to be the case, but I still glared at Wyatt since we were at our place of business.

"Seriously?" I asked.

"What? It's his new hashtag online. It's quite cute. What was that last model's name?"

"Miss Never Going to Get Her so stop thinking about that," Gabriel answered. "Although, I didn't sleep with her either. You know the media. Hell, you should definitely know the media with what Lark has to deal with."

I just shook my head and sipped my coffee. "Still

doesn't explain why you're up so early. Or have you not gone to bed yet?" I asked, brow raised.

Gabriel smiled like a cat in cream, and I sighed, wondering what the hell this kid was doing. Not that he was a kid anymore, but seriously. One day he was going to fuck up, and then we were going to have to deal with it. But for now, he seemed to be on the right course.

Wyatt, on the other hand, chuckled. "I was sleeping after not going to bed until after three because I closed last night, and now I'm exhausted because this asshole wanted me to wake up."

"You're the one who said I could sleep in your guest room. It's not my fault you're a light sleeper." Gabriel beamed and reached out for my coffee.

I smacked his hand away and glared. "My coffee. No touchy."

"You haven't seen that movie in how long, and you still quote it all?" Gabriel asked, his eyes dancing.

"It wasn't supposed to be a *llama*," I said deadpan as my brothers rolled their eyes, and we headed towards the hotel restaurant, the bagel I had eaten not enough after hearing about pancakes.

I was on paperwork duty today, so I ate pancakes with my brothers, nodded and talked to the rest of the Wilders as they came in and out, then headed to my office.

The scene of the crime, as it were.

Because even though this place had been cleaned the night before, and we had tidied up and made sure there was no evidence of what happened, I could still smell her.

Damn it. This was going to be a fucking problem.

I ignored that though, because I had work to do. And while Aurora was going to be on my mind after what happened, I had to focus on something else if I was going to survive this with my sanity intact. At least part of my sanity.

I had my door open, since I wasn't working on anything high priority or with sensitive information, so I could hear people walking back and forth, some of my family members heading to their offices, some bigwigs here for a retreat and renting out the conference room.

A knock at the door pulled my attention, and I blinked in surprise at who stood in the doorway, the bottom of my stomach falling.

I swallowed, my pen falling from my hand as I stood up, staring at Heather's parents. I couldn't believe they were here. Why were they here?

Justin White stood with a frown on his face, as his wife Laura White stood next to him, both of them looking as if they'd seen a ghost, but maybe they had. After all, I hadn't seen them since the funeral. The same funeral where they had shouted at me to leave because I was no longer welcome in their presence.

The Whites had never liked me. I hadn't married their daughter when they thought I should, and then I'd gotten her pregnant. Neither one of us thought that a piece of paper was going to change how we felt about one another. I worked in weddings day in and day out now, but I still felt like it was up to the couple or triad if they wanted to make it legal. If they wanted the big bash where they declared their love for each other in front of friends and family. If they wanted to go to the courthouse, or have a small picnic, I didn't fucking care. Heather and I wanted to do everything on our own terms, in our own time. And because of that, I hadn't been able to be there. I hadn't been able to go behind the closed doors of the hospital. I wasn't next of kin.

I was just the person left behind for her parents to blame.

"We heard that you had moved here, but I hadn't realized you worked here, too," Laura White said into the quiet. I wasn't sure what I was supposed to say to that. I wasn't sure if I was supposed to say anything.

"I own this place with my family. It's a Wilder company." My voice sounded dull.

Heather's father narrowed his gaze. "Then you've

landed on your feet. What do you do here? Run the business?"

"I help run security."

That was the worst thing I could have said, because Heather's father scoffed and looked over my head, as if he couldn't even bear the sight of me.

I didn't blame him. I couldn't stand the sight of me either sometimes.

"You protect people, but you couldn't protect her? It should have been you. Our baby girl's gone, and you couldn't protect her. You let all of this happen, and we'll never forgive you. You left town because you couldn't stand the guilt, and now you're here, thriving? How could you?"

"We should go. I can't even look at him," Justin grumbled.

"It should have been you! It should have been you!" Heather's mother wailed, and I couldn't say anything. I just let her scream.

I didn't even see Trace come in and pull her back.

"Ma'am. You're going to have to restrain yourself."

"Get your hands off my wife!"

I stepped forward, my hands outstretched. "Trace, you can let her go as long as they agree to leave."

"Are you sure, Ridge?"

"Don't you dare touch me. I'll sue you. I'll have this whole business in my hands," Laura spat.

"Come on, honey. We'll just leave, we don't need to stay here for the wedding."

Wedding? So they were here for someone's wedding. They hadn't realized it was at a place that had my last name? That was on them. But the bile rising up my throat, that was on me.

Trace gave me a look, letting me know that I would have to have answers later. The problem was I didn't have any.

Trace and two others of my team came and escorted them out, while I stood there, palms damp, hands shaking.

But then I realized I wasn't alone. Aurora was there, her face pale as she looked at me.

I didn't have any words for her. What the hell was I supposed to say that would make sense?

"Just go."

Aurora shook her head as she moved forward and closed the door behind her. It made a soft click that sounded like it was echoing in my head. I sat down in the visitor chair in front of the desk and moaned.

"Ridge. Who were they?" she asked softly, her hand tentatively touching my shoulder. I jerked away, not because it was her touch, just because it was any touch, and I looked up to see the hurt on her gaze before she blinked it away. Cursing, I reached out and gripped her hand.

"I'm sorry. You're not doing anything wrong. I just, I wasn't expecting to ever see them again. Let alone in my fucking office."

"Who were they, Ridge?"

"Nobody. Just people from my past."

"I've told you everything that happened with me. My past, and how it keeps coming up. For me, it helps to talk about it, but if it doesn't help you, I'll go. But I'm here if you need a shoulder. Or just someone to rant at."

I looked up at her, at the determination in her face, and I was just so tired.

"They are the parents of my dead girlfriend." She flinched at my flat tone, but I kept going.

"Heather and I had been dating for a couple of years, and her parents didn't like me because I wasn't a doctor or a lawyer or anything that made good money. I did okay for myself, didn't have any debt, and we were saving for a house. We lived together, loved each other. I was twenty minutes late to the homecoming parade."

Her eyes widened, and I realized that South Texas wasn't as big as people thought. Geographically it was fucking huge, but something like what I was about to say? That made the news. And people remembered.

"Oh, Ridge."

"She was waiting for me, annoyed, but it was fine. I kissed her as soon as I got there, said I was sorry, then the first shot rang out. The three men shot into the crowd because they hated people, or just wanted to make the news and go out in a blaze of glory, killed seven people. Eight in reality, though they don't count that in some numbers. One of the people they killed had been driving, and that car ran into the crowd. I pulled Heather out of the way of the car, afraid she was going to get hit, but I was too slow to stop the bullet. Or the second one. One slammed right into her chest, the other into her stomach. Where our unborn child was growing."

Tears were freely falling down her cheeks and I stood up, reaching to wipe them away.

"Her parents wouldn't even let me say goodbye. I couldn't go to her bedside, couldn't hear anything from the doctors because I wasn't family. I wasn't next of kin. It wasn't until they realized Heather had been pregnant that they actually let me hear anything because I was the father. I was barely allowed at the funeral, and I couldn't even stay in town to find out what they wanted to do to me next."

"How could they blame you for that act of hate? That wasn't you."

"For some reason they felt like if I had been there on time, we would have moved and not been in that position. Or if I would've used my skills and training to move her out of the way and not protect myself, their daughter would be alive. They need someone to hate, and it had to be me."

"And they can't hate the men who did that?"

"They can. But they only caught two of the guys. The third one ran off on foot, and they never found him. We don't even know what he did, how he was part of it, or who fired the shots that killed Heather. But they hate me, and I don't blame them. Sometimes I hate myself." I swallowed, the guilt hitting me hard. "It's been two and a half years. Two and a half years since the shooting, since my life changed. And I still think about her every day, just like you think of your William. But her parents? They hate me more and more. I can't change that. I don't even know if I should try." I sat down, my hands over my face as the tears came, and Aurora held me.

I didn't even realize that's what I wanted, what I needed, until her arms were around me, whispering sweet words I could barely understand. But she kept telling me it wasn't my fault. And while a part of me believed that, it was hard for all of me to.

I pulled her into my lap, needing to hold her a bit

closer. She curled into me, and I held her close as I let it all out.

"It's not your fault."

"I know," I whispered. We were silent for long enough my chest ached more, but finally I let out another breath. "But sometimes it feels like it."

"I know about guilt. We both know that. But you're not alone. And I have a feeling your family doesn't know?"

I shook my head, my forehead against hers.

"Tell them, Ridge. They deserve to know."

"I know. I need to. I will. Once I figure out what to do."

"Well, with what just happened, I don't think you're going to have a choice soon." I just held her after that; we didn't kiss, didn't do anything beyond holding each other.

Because that was the first time I'd ever laid it all out. Ever let myself do so.

And the fact that it was with Aurora? The fact that I felt safe enough to do that? That meant something.

What? I didn't know. But I had a feeling I was going to find out.

CHAPTER ELEVEN
AURORA

Music blared through the speakers as I swayed my hips to the beat, piping bag in hand and a smile on my lips. While part of me wanted to say this good mood was because of who I had woken up with that morning and *how* we'd woken up, the honest part of me knew it was because of the cake currently looking like the pièce de resistance of my entire baking career.

Sex and emotions were nice.

But sometimes cake was better.

I must have had a little too much sugar and caffeine and not enough vegetables because sex with Ridge was *far* better than cake.

However, looking at the pretty floral work and *knowing* I'd kicked it up a notch from my usual.

That was freaking fantastic.

I stood back and smiled at the cake. It was a salted caramel cake with a decadent fluffy and moist interior with rich buttery filling. I had added oozes of salted caramel for an extra delight. Just a touch of salt made it intensely amazing, if I did say so myself. I had made a set of pistachio cupcakes earlier, and I was thrilled with how they turned out. The dessert for the restaurant tonight was a raspberry chocolate truffle cake, which had been fun to make. Later I'd be working on a carrot cake, as well as peanut butter cupcakes for a baby shower. Tomorrow I had a Bananas Foster cake and a red velvet cake with cream cheese frosting scheduled to bake. And then later this week I was making a coffee cake with vanilla espresso buttercream, and a caramel apple cake. Next week I got to play with an Earl Grey and vanilla bean buttercream, and then a lemon elder-flower cake.

My mouth was watering just thinking about all of that, plus I had a tasting with the pistachio and the salted caramel and a hazelnut praline as well as a vanilla latte with a fresh raspberry jam. I loved my job, and I loved working with clients and figuring out their perfect cakes. Because many of the weddings were big enough to need more than one cake, I got to do cupcakes and desserts and cream cakes as well. That meant a lot of flavors, but a lot of hard work that I could take pride in.

My stomach rumbled, and I realized that I'd only had cake and coffee most of the day. It was time for me to eat a real meal and take care of myself.

"My mouth is watering just looking at that," Kendall said from behind me, and I looked over my shoulder and smiled.

"I am pretty proud of myself with this one. Now I just need to make the caramel-covered praline shards and shoots, and it'll be ready to go."

"That won't take you that long at all."

"And then I head over to the photographer, and the staff will be cutting it so I don't have to be there, which is good because we have a long list to work through."

My stomach rumbled again, and Kendall raised a brow. "You know I do make food that can feed you. You're allowed to eat."

I blushed, then went right back to work, finishing up the last bits by dipping the walnuts and almonds in homemade caramel and stringing out the ends to make perfect shards. Thankfully it wasn't a hot day so this wasn't going to melt, but we would still have to be quick about it.

"I'm almost done, I promise. And then I will eat all the things."

"As long as you're taking care of yourself." Kendall paused, and I looked over at her for a minute before putting my attention back on the hot caramel so I wouldn't injure myself.

"What is it? Is there something you need, or am I doing something wrong?" I winced as soon as I said the words, knowing they weren't coming from anything recent, but from my own past experiences. It wasn't their fault that I had worked with people who ended up hating me. Who had reminded me day in and day out that it should have been me who died and not their precious son. I understood their pain, but not their anger at me. It hadn't been my fault. Therapy had helped me learn that. But they would never understand.

"No, you're doing wonderful. You are the best addition we've had here in a while. And that's saying something because I'm very selfish when it comes to my kitchen. And we've had some amazing additions. I'm so happy that you're here."

I finished up the last shard and looked over at her while wiping my hands on my towel.

"What is it?" I asked, suddenly concerned.

"I know you're trying to probably keep this secret, but I saw the way you and Ridge looked at each other."

I froze, the towel slipping from my hand before I forced myself to catch it.

"Oh. *Oh.* Well, I guess I don't know the rules?" I asked, my voice going high-pitched at the end. "With work, and I guess the family. Well...I'm just going to... well. Never mind." I turned to clean up my station, while the staff members—who thankfully hadn't been listening to the conversation thanks to their head-phones—moved to take the cake away.

I waved at it, knowing that no matter how much work I put into it, it would soon be dismantled.

"No, that's not what I'm saying," Kendall said after they left and put her hand on my shoulder. I turned to look at her and saw the distress on her face.

"I'm happy for you. I was more worried that if you wanted to keep it secret, you two should probably stop giving each other long looks whenever you are in the same room or near each other. Because we've noticed. At least the girls. I have no idea if the Wilder men have figured it out yet. And I don't even know what *it* is. We just know there are looks. I'm curious and I totally want to know everything, but I know you probably need some time to think about it, so I'm going to let you have that. But, well, I figured you should know."

I blinked at her, wondering what the answer was here. Because I didn't have any. Of course, people would figure it out. I couldn't keep my emotions off my face when it came to Ridge, not that I even knew what those emotions were. I saw the way he looked at me. I could still remember his taste. It only made sense that people would figure it out. I just hadn't thought beyond our own needs and desires. Our own fledgling...*whatever* this was.

"I don't really know what to say other than I'm sorry."

"Please don't be sorry. Seeing you smile, seeing *Ridge* smile? It's amazing. And we don't have a workplace rule against dating," Kendall started. "It'd be mighty hypocritical of us, considering how many of the Wilders have married people that work here."

"Oh, it's not, it's really not that," I said, putting both hands up.

Kendall snorted. "I know. If that happened, I would sit you down and ask if you needed to take a break. No one needs to get married after, what, three weeks of knowing each other? Maybe more. Oh, has time flown by."

I swallowed hard. "Tell me about it. But no, it's not that. I just, well, I have no idea what this thing is or what it will be or what it could be. I'm just enjoying myself. Which is something I haven't done in a long while. And I don't want Ridge to feel pressured. Especially because we work in a place surrounded by weddings and happiness and, well, that is totally not on the table."

Kendall met my gaze and studied my face before she nodded. "Okay. Take your time. Just know that I don't think it's as secret as you want it to be. And we are very nosy. We want to know everything. But we'll give you some time. Just a little bit of time." She put her two fingers together, barely letting light through.

I laughed and shook my head. "It's good to know about the workplace rule, or lack thereof. And I guess I'll have an awkward conversation with Ridge about the fact that his cousins and brothers will probably figure things out soon if they haven't already."

Kendall beamed. "They probably don't know. They'd already be annoying all of us if they did. We women are a little quicker. We figured it out, but we'll give you some space. Until we don't. Because one day I will attack you with wine and cheese and will want to know it all." She winked as she said it, and then moved my shoulder so I faced the door. "Go eat. Go see if a certain Wilder is on break so you can eat with him. Get out of here." Then she pushed me out of the kitchen, and I laughed, wondering how I had made a friend so quickly. I had already told Joni all about her, and Joni was ecstatic for me. There wasn't a jealous bone in Joni's body. She would never be annoyed that I was making new friends, and she was even over-joyed that I was actually trying. Leaving the house, baking things that I loved, and getting away from the memories that never seemed to end. I counted that as a win.

I said my goodbyes and cleaned up after myself before I headed to pick up something to eat from the employee area. And as if I had conjured him into exis-tence, Ridge was there, an energy drink in hand and a brow raised.

"Hey," I said, suddenly feeling awkward about seeing him, especially after the conversation I'd just had. He must have seen something on my face because he tilted his head and gave me a look.

"What's wrong?"

I shook my head. "Nothing."

He moved forward, putting his thumb under my chin.

"What's wrong?"

There was something about the command in his voice, that deepness that sent a little thrill through me. There was probably something wrong with me and I didn't care.

"First, I haven't eaten all day so I'm starving, but also, I just had a very weird conversation with Kendall."

Ridge's eyes widened. "Well, let's get you something to eat, and then we can talk about what she said."

I shook my head. "You have to get back to work. I know this isn't your lunch break."

"I can take a few minutes."

"Let me just grab something quick. And what she said wasn't bad, it was just that I believe the female subgroup of the Wilder clan knows. They don't know everything, but they know that you and I are...well, doing what we're doing."

And now that I said that out loud, it sounded ridiculous. Maybe labels were important to prevent you from sounding like a dumbass when you were speaking.

Ridge let his hand fall before he started to laugh and shook his head.

"I suppose that makes sense. They know everything that goes on around here, even if we pretend we're the ones that do."

I bit my lip. "I'm sorry. I know we haven't talked about it, or what exactly is going on, and I know it's no one's business but, well, there you go."

"Hell." He ran his hands through his hair, making it slightly messy, and way too sexy for his own good. There was seriously something wrong with me in this moment.

"Is your only response to this going to be to laugh?" I asked, wanting to laugh with him but still feeling a little nervous.

Ridge moved forward and cupped my cheek before he leaned down and brushed his lips against mine. Anyone could be walking down the corridor, then again anyone could have walked in when we had had sex in his office. We weren't really hiding it very well, were we?

He leaned back and pressed his lips to my cheek before lowering his hand and giving me a look.

"We're fine. I'm just surprised it took them this long. I'm not surprised however that they knew before we did that we were together."

I wanted to ask him what he meant by together. But then again, this wasn't the time or place to ask. And I wasn't sure I wanted to know the answer. Because what exactly did he want? If I didn't know what I wanted, why was I allowed to know what he wanted? After all this time it was nice just to be. That wasn't something I allowed myself to do often these days.

"Hey, Ridge, we need you," Trace said from down the hallway, and Ridge stiffened before he looked over. "On my way."

"It's nothing serious, Aurora. You don't have to be worried. Promise."

I blushed but shook my head as Ridge opened his mouth to say something, but I interrupted him. "Let me go eat. I'll see you later?"

He studied my face, then leaned down and kissed me again. "Yeah. I'll see you later."

And then he was gone, and I felt even more confused than before. Or maybe not at all. Maybe this was exactly what it needed to be. Just moments like this, precious ones, stolen ones, and eventually I'd figure out exactly what I wanted.

I wasn't sure it was going to be Ridge Wilder. Wasn't sure I wanted it to be Ridge Wilder. Not when he already did something to me just by breathing.

He ran off, all strong and protective to do something to literally protect the people here. And now I needed to go eat something quick and go back to baking and making sure people's memories and moments were as perfect as they wanted them to be.

I wanted to kiss him again. I wanted to be with him again. I just wasn't sure what either one of us could take beyond that. Because it had been enough time, according to some people, for us both to move on. But he still hadn't told his family about his loss. They didn't know he was grieving. So how did I fit in his life?

And when was I allowed to ask?

I didn't have the right. I knew that. Just like I knew

we would never use the word "replace" when talking about either of our losses. Because we were coming to this label, whatever it was, from similar pasts. Because William was always going to be here. Just like Heather would always be here. They would always be in this relationship, whether we wanted it or not. And I didn't think that was a bad thing.

I just didn't know what that meant in the long term.

Or whether it needed to be long term at all.

I was talking myself in circles, so I shook my head and went to get something to eat before heading back to the kitchen. Because that's what I needed to focus on. Things I could fix, things I could make better.

Not things that might break me. I had just pieced myself back together. And I wasn't sure I could do that a second time.

CHAPTER TWELVE
RIDGE

Me: *Dinner tomorrow?*

Aurora: *It depends on how late the wedding runs. I'm still at the pink event now.*

Me: *See you after? In case dinner tomorrow doesn't work?*

There was a long enough pause that I was afraid that I was going too hard too fast. I didn't know why I was even asking this. I didn't know where I stood with Aurora, other than the fact that we connected far too quickly. She made me want to open up, to be better. I didn't understand exactly how we'd gotten here. I wasn't sure where we were going.

Aurora: *Okay. And there's a chance tonight could be going to be a long night*

Me: *If you need help, let me know. I can get out of this.*

Aurora: *Excuse me? No. This is your brother time. You know Wyatt was looking forward to dinner with the four of you after all this time. The other Wilders and I have the wedding and property taken care of. Enjoy your time with your brothers.*

I wondered how she understood the situation so quickly. But she did. She knew what I felt, and not just because I told her some of it. She just understood. I'd never met someone that understood me like that. We were so good about not discussing what that meant. We were in our own little bubble here on the Wilder property. Between me living here and working here, and us being able to find food here often, we rarely left the place. But in the weeks since the wedding where we had met, we had settled into a routine. We ate dinner together when we could, mostly at my cabin. I had been to her place a couple of times, but it was easier to be here. Easier to see each other on our lunch breaks, for me to come visit her when she was working on a big cake. And I really liked cake.

It made sense that we would stay here, rather than leave and go anywhere else. That was going to have to change, I knew. She deserved that. Whatever this was between us, she deserved being taken out and not feeling like she was being hidden. Not that I was hiding her.

Only, I wasn't quite sure if I was ready to show her off.

And that was on me.

Me: *I'll text you when we are done. Have fun. And save me some cake.*

Aurora: *Of course, I have cake for you. And I would say something suggestive about that, but we both know that I'm still too new at this whole thing to.*

I laughed, said my goodbyes, and then looked up to see Gabriel staring at me.

"What?" I asked after a moment since Gabriel hadn't said anything.

"So." He drew out the word. "Who are you texting?"

"I don't know why that's any of your business." I slid my phone into my pocket, and Wyatt came over, finger pointing at me.

"Aha!"

"What? Why the hell are you pointing at me?"

"It's a girl. You have to be talking to a girl."

Brooks came out, a towel in his hands as he dried them off. "Is he finally going to spill about Aurora? Because us pretending that we don't know that they're together or banging or whatever they are doing is getting quite annoying."

I looked between the three of them and pinched the bridge of my nose. "Are you serious right now? You want to talk about what, my feelings? Aurora? Or can we just go and eat and stop prying in my life?"

"Aha," Wyatt repeated.

"Stop saying that. It makes no sense."

"It makes perfect sense. You now have a life. Aurora has ensured that. We need to know when this happened, and what your prospects are, and just tell us everything."

I looked between my three brothers and wondered exactly why I had decided that having all of us live near each other, at least when Gabriel was in town, and work with each other was a smart idea. Just because it worked for our cousins didn't mean it would work for us. I should have just nipped this in the bud and stopped the whole thing. But no, I had wanted family time. And now I was paying for those decisions.

They all began to talk at once and I held up my hands. "Seriously, how is this any of your business?"

"Because it should be." Gabriel shrugged and leaned back in his chair. "You all moved here, with me being the occasional guest, so we could get to know one another. To be in each other's business. So let us be. Tell us. What are you and Aurora doing? Can you finally talk about it? Is it serious? Are you dating? Are you just sleeping with each other? Are you going to break that poor widow's heart like you told me I wasn't allowed to do? Tell us."

"Everything he said," Wyatt put in as he popped a tomato in his mouth from the antipasto tray on the table.

I sat down on a chair across from them, put my elbows on my knees, and then covered my face with my hands.

"I really don't have time for this now."

"See, I think you're lying. I think you have all the time in the world."

"I don't know what's going on between us. We're just enjoying each other's company." That sounded as if that was the best I was going to come up with, but Gabriel just rolled his eyes.

"That sounds like the copout I use when I'm trying to talk to anyone but the press." My youngest brother sighed. "Of course, when I do talk to the press, I say nothing. Because that's exactly what the answers are."

"So, you haven't slept with every single person the media assumes you have?" Wyatt asked, snagging a piece of prosciutto.

"Of course not. I think my dick would fall off after all that use. Don't you?"

"I don't tend to think about your dick," Brooks answered before he reached out for an olive.

I looked between the three of them and figured dick talk and all, that this was why we moved to be near each other. Yes, I knew we were probably all running from our own demons, but the closeness was why we were here. So maybe it was time I actually talked about more than just what was going on with Aurora and me.

"I don't know what's going on with me and Aurora, but I'm not going to hurt her. Because she's not the only one who's lost someone."

They all froze and stared at me. Brooks paled and took a seat hard next to Gabriel.

"What do you mean?" Brooks asked, and I knew I probably should have told him separately. But then again, maybe he would need our brothers soon, just like I did in this moment.

"Aurora lost her husband. Like you all know. And it's been five years and we're doing what we're doing. I don't know what it means, I don't know how serious it is. But I need to tell you guys about Heather."

"Who's Heather?" Gabriel asked, his voice so soft I barely heard it over the roaring in my ears. It felt as if someone were tearing up my heart and taking whatever pulp was left and smashing it into the carpet below. I hadn't felt this kind of pain when it came to Heather in so long that it felt new again. I knew that I would never be over Heather. But I had learned to grow. To be strong.

But in that moment I felt weak.

"Heather was my girlfriend, up north. Before I moved here. We had been together for a couple of years."

"She's the girl you mentioned in passing," Wyatt said, his brows furrowed. "I had forgotten about her. Mostly because we were all dealing with our own shit, and I just thought you broke up. What happened to Heather, Ridge?"

I swallowed hard, my hands shaking. It was Brooks that stood up, Brooks who had lost someone that he loved with all of his heart. My brother stood and gripped my shoulder, keeping me steady.

This was why I moved here. To be with my family. Aurora was right, I had needed to tell them. To open up. Because how were they supposed to know I had been dying inside all along if I didn't tell them?

"Heather died about six months before we moved here. She's *why* I moved here."

And as I went into the details, of the shooter, the car, the baby, I knew I should have told them long before this. But I was afraid that saying it aloud would make it real. Telling the people that I loved more than anything in the world would make it real.

And I hadn't wanted it to be.

"Why the hell didn't you tell us?" Wyatt asked, the anger in his tone brittle.

"I didn't know how."

"Because you thought we were weak? That we'd break? We could have been there for you." Gabriel ran his hands over his face. "I mean, you guys moved here and I've been here as much as I could over the years, but it still wasn't enough. How could we not know? You lost everything and we didn't know."

Brooks's grip tightened on my shoulder, and I whistled out a breath through my teeth.

"You should have told us. You were there for me when I lost her. You should have told us."

I swallowed hard but couldn't look up and meet my brother's gaze. There was no excuse for keeping this from them for as long as I had that they would believe.

"I know. I know. I just didn't know how. And then so much time passed and I thought I was better but I realized I wasn't. But you guys being here? It's everything. And I know we're all fucking hiding our own secrets. We're all hiding our own pain and all that shit and I get it. But maybe we need to be like our cousins and actually open up. I can't believe I'm the one that's saying things like this."

"Honestly, I'm also surprised you are the one saying that," Wyatt said, the pain in his eyes mixing with something else I couldn't quite read. "I'm sorry. I'm so damn sorry. I really would have liked to meet her. And your kid. Which sounds terrible now that I'm saying it out loud. So I have no idea what I'm supposed to be saying." He looked over at Gabriel. "You're the one that is the writer. What should we say?"

Gabriel just looked at us, his eyes wide. "I don't have the words. Shit, Ridge. I'm sorry. And can I just say, if this isn't weird, the fact that you seem to be opening up to Aurora, or maybe you being with Aurora in whatever way that you are means that you can open up to us? I mean, fucking fall in love with that woman. Just saying."

Brooks burst out laughing and I grinned, grateful for that break in the tension.

"That wasn't awkward as fucking hell," Brooks said through tears of laughter.

I wiped my face, knowing that my tears had nothing to do with humor, and leaned back into the chair. "Aurora told me I needed to tell you. Because it wasn't fair to any of us to keep secrets that big. But once you've kept them for so long, it is hard to break through that. So, I'm going to do better."

"Meaning you're going to tell us how you feel about Aurora?" Wyatt asked, and I knew he was deflecting, and I was grateful. But I wasn't about to answer.

I threw an olive at him, and he caught it and tossed it in his mouth. I sighed, and then the subject was closed. I would bring up Heather again, and I knew they would, too. But we had finally talked about it. They knew. I wasn't harboring this secret anymore. That had to count for something.

And maybe I did have Aurora to thank.

I wasn't quite sure what that meant. Or if I wanted it to mean anything at all.

By the time we finished dinner, I had told them a few stories about Heather, ones that made them laugh, and I felt lighter because of it. I had hidden her from them, hidden from my own pain, and that was a disservice to Heather's memory. I promised myself I would do better going forward. I just wasn't sure what I should do next.

It was late, and when I texted Aurora I was home, I hoped she was already home. Not that I didn't want to see her, just that I knew she'd had a long day. But I had heard the party still going strong on the other side of the property, so I figured she might still be on property. I hoped she would have texted me if she left earlier, but I knew she was likely still working hard.

Aurora: *Good timing. I just finished up and was figuring out if I was going to head home or not. I'm exhausted, and Kendall said there's a room for me if I wanted it.*

I immediately texted back.

Me: *Get over here. You are not sleeping in the inn.*

Aurora: *Bossy. But okay. I'll be right there.*

I smiled at that, wondering when everything had changed, or perhaps it hadn't. Perhaps this was the same no promises.

It took her less than five minutes, and I was already opening the door when she walked up, her large bag in hand.

"It's my overnight bag in case I need to stay over for a cake emergency. I promise I'm not making assumptions here."

I gripped the back of her neck and brought her to me.

"Stop overthinking this."

"But I'm very good at overthinking."

I closed the door behind her and then my mouth was on hers.

"I see you tasted some of that pistachio cake," I said with a laugh as I leaned back.

"Well, I did pack away some for you." I realized that her other hand was holding a paper bag, so I took both bags and headed towards the kitchen.

"I'm going to put the cake in the fridge, so I don't accidentally knock it off the counter when I kiss you."

She blushed as I lowered my head, taking her lips with mine. When I finally pulled away, we were both panting, and she smiled up at me. "How was dinner with your brothers?"

I leaned forward, gripped her hips, and kissed her hard.

"Dinner was great. I told them everything, but I don't want to get into it right now. I just need you. Is that all right? Just you and me for the night?"

She studied my face for a moment before a bright smile slid over her features.

"I think that sounds like the perfect way to end a very long day." Then she went up on her tiptoes and kissed me back.

I tugged her hair, deepening the kiss. She moaned into me, and then I started slowly walking her backwards towards the bedroom. When I couldn't take it any longer, I picked her up and carried her the rest of the way, needing her in there as quickly as possible. She wrapped her arms around my neck, kissing and nibbling along my jaw. I growled, then very nearly tossed her on the bed. I refrained at the last instant and set her on her feet. Before she could say anything, I kissed her again, pulling at the buttons on her shirt. She tugged on the bottom of mine, and then we were wrestling, falling to the bed as we stripped each other. Laughter burst from both of us, but there were few words, mostly just feelings.

"Ridge."

"I'm here. I've got you."

Soon we were both naked, my hands between her thighs, my middle finger over her clit as I spread her swollen folds. She was so wet and so hot already. It was only a matter of time, a few moments before she would come on my hand. Then, of course, her hand was on my cock, squeezing the base of the shaft before she slid it up and down, taking her time with me.

"I've got you. I've got you." I slid one finger deep inside her and she came, shaking on my hand as she arched back. I moved over her, reaching for the condom. As she helped me with it, we slid our hands over each other. I lowered my head, taking one nipple into my mouth, then the other. Her breasts were large enough to overfill my hand, and I continued to play with her as I settled myself between her legs. I moved back, pressing her legs up so her knees were by her shoulders. She grinned as I sank deep inside. We both moaned, and then I was moving, forcing her to hold her legs open for me as I held her down, going harder, faster, needier.

When her body began to shake, I pulled out of her and flipped her over to her knees, sliding back into her as she leaned back onto my chest. She was so tight, so hot, that I could barely breathe, could barely think. All I wanted was to be with her. She came again, my one hand on her breast and the other down on her clit. I followed her, biting down on her shoulder so I wouldn't scream her name. So I wouldn't accidentally shout something that meant too much. Because I didn't know what I wanted. What I could handle.

She was so sweet, so soft. She was just putting herself back together. I didn't want to be the one to break her. And I wasn't sure I could be the one to keep her safe.

Because as we fell into each other, I knew I could fall in love with her. And that would be a problem.

Especially when it might be too late.

I hadn't kept the person that I loved before alive. Hadn't kept her safe.

I wasn't sure what would happen if I failed again.

CHAPTER THIRTEEN
AURORA

I slid down the bed, my knees cushioned on a pillow as Ridge ran his fingers through my hair. When I gripped the base of his shaft, he groaned, tugging on my hair gently.

"This is a nice way to wake up," he growled, and I smiled against his cock before I opened my mouth and hovered over the tip. He kept his hips in place, not pushing forward, and from the way his thighs strained I knew he wanted to. So I filled my mouth with him, letting my tongue tease along the bottom of his cock as the head touched the back of my throat. I couldn't swallow him all, so I gripped his shaft base and squeezed.

"Aurora," he groaned,

I hummed around his mouthful, careful to not graze my teeth against him.

"Jesus Christ," he grumbled, and I kept going, sucking on him, taking him. I was in control here, I needed the control.

It had been so long since I had done anything like this, it was almost like I was having to relearn how to do this correctly, how to enjoy this. But it was everything. It was exactly what I wanted, what I needed.

I hadn't realized that I had been missing moments like these, when I was the one who held him in place.

But this was everything.

He pulled at my hair again and I looked up at him, licking my lips. He reached down and slid his thumb over the wetness of my mouth.

"So fucking beautiful. You want me to come down that throat of yours? Or maybe all over those pretty tits." He slid his thumb in and out of my mouth, mimicking the action I had just done, and I rounded my lips, sucking hard. He smirked at me before sliding his thumb out.

"What do you want, baby?"

"You."

A simple answer with so much hidden beneath the words.

Because here there was power, here there was need. Here there were moments for just the two of us.

Instead of letting me go down on him again, he

tugged at my shoulders and cupped my face. He was so gentle, so sweet. It was hard to believe that this was the same man who had nearly broken us when we reached for each other throughout the night and fell off the bed in laughter as we succumbed to each other.

This wasn't what I had expected when I had started working here. Nor had I thought this was where a social media post would lead. And yet I couldn't imagine myself any other place.

This was fun, this was lovely, and this was probably becoming too much.

I didn't want to fall for him. Not so soon, not when I didn't even know what I wanted. I just wanted to live in this moment.

He flipped me onto my back, spread my legs, and I watched his head dive between my legs as he spread my folds and began to lick.

My back arched and I covered my breasts with my hands, pinching my own nipples, playing with myself just like he liked.

It shocked me that I already knew him so well. So quickly.

And yet, in the end, maybe we had always been meant to be here.

I didn't want to think about that, I couldn't. I couldn't let this be more than it was.

Then I couldn't think about anything anymore because he was licking me, spreading me, and I was coming, my toes curling over his shoulders, his palm on my stomach to keep me pinned as he kept licking me through it.

"Your whole body turns this rosy pink when you come. It's so fucking hot." He licked my wetness off his lips and reached for the condom. I helped him slide it on, and we moved so he sat at the edge of the bed and I straddled him. With his feet planted on the floor and mine planted on the bed behind him, I sat on his lap and he lifted me by the hips, and slowly slid me down over his cock.

"So fucking tight," he gritted out. I didn't have any words because he was so damn big.

"Keep going. Just for me. Keep going."

I smiled, lifting myself up with his help as he rocked into me. In this position he was so deep it was hard to even think, but we kept moving, and I tried to keep my breath, and then suddenly I was coming, my body shaking, as I clamped down around him.

He met my gaze and groaned, my name a whisper on his lips as he came, keeping me steady over his cock as we both tried to come down from our orgasms, but I wasn't sure if I would ever be the same again. Not after last night, and not after this.

He pushed my hair back from my face, neither of us moving from our position. He smiled at me softly, and I thought I saw a newness there. A gentleness underneath the harsh growls of Ridge Wilder.

"Good morning."

I smiled wide, sweaty and somewhat sore, but in the best way possible.

"Good morning."

"Well, that's probably my favorite way to wake up. Though I think we're both running late."

My eyes widened as I looked over his shoulder at the clock and tried to scramble off him, though it was kind of difficult with us in this particular position.

"We'll get there. It's okay. I am one of the bosses."

"But not my boss."

"Only last night." He winked, then bit my lip before we were laughing and falling on top of each other.

Needless to say, we were late for work.

But only a little bit.

At the end of the day, I had finally gotten the last bits of frosting out of my hair and glared at my reflection in the mirror.

"Well, I'm so glad that I did my hair today. What's a little frosting between friends."

Kendall snorted from behind me. "Once I ended up with bouillabaisse on me, and I'm still not quite sure how that happened. But it went everywhere, and I was so mad because it took so freaking long to make the damn thing."

"Oh, I can only imagine. At least frosting is ready to be eaten. Albeit not out of my hair."

Kendall reached over and wiped more off my chin and I cursed.

"Is your family going to be okay that this is how I look for the girl time wine-and-cheese extravaganza?"

I sounded high-pitched and excited, but I was so damn nervous, because this was Ridge's family. These were the women who married into the Wilders.

And now I would be hanging out with them, having wine, cheese, and pretending somehow that I fit in. Because apparently the entire family knew that Ridge and I were dating?

Dating worked. That was a good name for what we were doing. We were together. Nothing serious, nothing where we would actually discuss our feelings and futures, but enough that now I was having wine and cheese with the girls before I had to head out for my errands. Just a quick hour break with the women that I worked with, and Ridge's family.

No pressure.

"Get out of your head. You look great. And it's just a

fun way to relax. Lark and Bethany are still out of town, so you don't have the full force of us."

I turned, raising a brow. "So, you're admitting that you're a force?"

"Of course we are, then again, you're part of us. Because you work here, and we're a family. You being with Ridge? That just adds a little more fun for us to go over."

I bit my lip. "How much do you want out of me?"

Kendall put her arm around my shoulders as we walked down the path to one of the staff golf carts. The winery was on the other side of the property so we could walk there, but it would be easier if we made our way on the golf cart. Plus, we'd be able to make it back quick so I could head to the grocery store before going home. I knew many of the Wilders used to live on property, though not all of them did now. So us having a break together before we all disbanded to go about our normal routines would be nice.

"Seriously though, you only have to tell us however much you want to. Though we do pry. And since Bethany and Lark are out of town, it's just you, me, Alexis, Maddie, and Sidney."

I bit my lip as Kendall rounded a corner, going a little too fast in my opinion, but considering I'd seen this woman drive, I wasn't surprised.

"Okay, so Alexis is the wedding planner for all of the events, and then Maddie does what? She's in charge of the wine club?"

Kendall nodded as we took another turn and I held on to the oh-shit bar on the golf cart.

Kendall smirked before she answered. "She is the director of the tasting room and the wine club manager and works alongside her husband Elijah who is the operations director. My Evan is the wine making director, so they all work closely together. As Amos is the senior manager. It's nice to have him around too, though he hasn't married into the Wilders yet. More's the pity."

I snorted. "And that means Elliot as the event manager works with Alexis day in and day out."

"Yep. And East works with everyone as he is in charge of maintenance and quality control along with Ridge's brother, Brooks. Wyatt runs the Wilder Barn Distillery on the other side. Which you need to go to if you haven't."

I shook my head. "No, it's not that I haven't wanted to see everything, I've just been a little hesitant about stepping into Ridge's brothers' activities, since they don't have anything to do with my job."

Kendall parked and we hopped out of the golf cart. She turned and smiled at me.

"I understand. It makes total sense. It is a little funny though because you do work with the rest of us."

"I don't know, I just feel like there's a demarcation line. Or I've lost my mind."

"Maybe. Okay, who am I missing?" Kendall asked as we walked inside the winery, and I looked around at the beautiful dark wood furniture and archways, and the random barrels artfully placed. It was soon to be after hours and the final tour was going through, which was how Maddie could come to this, so it was quiet and beautiful. Wine bottles and wine glasses were everywhere, but all in pristine condition. I had no idea how they did this, but considering how many people worked here, it made sense.

"Oh, duh, there is Everett who is our CFO, and Eli who is the CEO. Someone needed to fill those jobs, so they got to get the titles, but everybody's equal. Including the cousins, now that they bought that piece of land west of us and connected it."

I frowned. "I didn't know that. Why didn't I know that?"

"Because God forbid three of those brothers ever say that they did something and have pride in it. Gabriel? Oh, he'll shout to the rooftops because that's his personality."

"Gabriel Wilder. The rockstar."

Kendall rolled her eyes. "It took nearly a year of me knowing Evan for him to mention that his baby cousin was *the* Gabriel Wilder. I mean, Wilder's a common name. I just hadn't realized that it was that Gabriel."

"I had such a crush on him when I was a teenager. Not that I'm actually ever going to tell Ridge that."

"Tell Ridge what?" Sidney asked as she bounced through the doorway. She had on a floral crown. I smiled at her and pointed to the top of her head.

She blushed and quickly took it off.

"Why'd you do that? It looks beautiful."

"I was trying on different ones, and this was a failure since the color matching was off, but I accidentally kept it on."

"So the flower girls decided on floral wreaths?" Alexis asked as she came through the door with a tray of wine in hand.

Maddie nearly barreled into her and scowled as she said, "Pregnant women do not carry trays." She took the tray away and served everybody our wine.

"This is a lovely pinot noir, rich, full bodied, with a slightly sweet taste so it's not too overpowering before you eat later."

"Salud," I said, and Maddie beamed as we all clicked glasses.

Maddie was right about the taste, and I swallowed

a bit before I found myself with a small plate of cheese and fruit that Kendall had prepared, and I just shook my head.

"You guys don't let a girl down at all."

"Of course not. We want you to be taken care of so you can tell us all the details."

"Speaking of details, flower girls?" Alexis asked again, and everybody laughed. "What? I need notes."

"I don't have the answer yet. They want to see these versus the roses. I said that they could do both, but the mother-in-law was very clear."

Alexis rolled her eyes. "Oh, very clear is a lovely phrase to use when you're talking about Clarice McButton."

"I have so many questions about that name."

Everyone looked at me and I blushed. "I don't know, McButton?"

"Of the *Oil McButtons*." Alexis rolled her eyes again. "We don't discuss the McButtons. Clarice though? That does sound like a serial killer."

"Right?" Kendall added.

"As in, I'm going to wear your skin and eat your liver with some fava beans?" I asked, laughing.

Everybody shuddered before Maddie snapped her fingers. "And he said chianti wrong and that has always bugged me."

I settled back as everyone spoke. I felt safe. This was nice, and I just felt as if things made sense. I ate cheese and drank wine as we talked about the days of work, the kids, and the upcoming concert that Lark was having in downtown San Antonio that they were all going to.

"We have the president's box by the way, so you're coming." I looked at Maddie who just grinned. "We're all the bossy ones here, so you have to listen to us."

"Well, that's a little scary. But sure."

"We really are nice, I promise," Sidney put in. "Much better than working at my last job." She shuddered as she sat and I reached over to clink my glass to hers.

"Cheers to that."

She took another drink as I took mine, and Alexis leaned forward.

"I thought you were working out of your house, right? Baking those amazing cookies that I love."

I blushed as everyone's attention turned to me. "For the past few years, yes. Because my sister-in-law kicked me out of the business."

I quickly explained about Lauren and my husband and everything that had happened that landed me in the position I was in. When they all started to curse Lauren for me, I wiped away a tear.

"We didn't mean to make you sad," Sidney said.

I sniffed and smiled at her. "I'm not sad. Not really. It's just nice to have you all out here protecting me. Same with Ridge." I set down my wine glass as everybody made a little tittering sound.

"And that's enough wine for me."

"Totally not enough wine," Maddie said as she held up the bottle.

"I have to drive home, and I need to make sure that I hit the grocery store first. So, no more wine."

"That makes perfect sense. But I have sparkling water for you," Maddie added.

I grinned. "That sounds perfect. And I don't want to talk about Ridge," I said.

"Oh, I think you should totally talk about Ridge." Alexis leaned forward. "You don't need to tell us everything, but we don't know much about the cousins. I mean, they've been working here for two years, and while Wyatt is outgoing and I absolutely adore him, Ridge just lurks."

"He works with one of my husbands, and yet I barely speak with him," Sidney added.

"Brooks is much the same way," Kendall said as she poured my water for me. I nodded in thanks and took a quick sip of the cold and sparkling water.

"I don't know much about them. I mean, I've

learned more about you guys and your husbands in the past hour than I have this whole time I've been working here. I guess everything just started all at once and it got a little confusing. I don't want to pressure Ridge into telling me all of his family's connections and secrets. Because I don't get to earn those."

"But you know Ridge. You know some of his secrets," Sidney said softly, and I swallowed hard and realized that everyone in this room knew too. Of course they did. Because their husbands knew, and these women were in healthy, loving relationships.

"I do. And I don't know. I don't know where it's going to lead. And I don't want to think too much about it because then I worry and I don't like to do that. So I'm just going to go with it, and I'm going to have fun. And I am not going to get hurt. Because that's not what either of us want."

"That sounds like the perfect way to handle this. And I'm proud of you. And no matter what, you're one of us. You're one of the girls that work with the Wilders."

As she said that Naomi walked in, her eyes puffy and her hair piled on the top of her head.

"Sorry I'm late, long day."

Alexis cursed under her breath and stood up, bringing Naomi into her arms.

"What is it?"

"Amos and I broke up. But it's fine. Totally fine. I could use some wine."

And then Naomi burst into tears, and I stood back with Sidney as the others pulled Naomi into a group hug, and I hoped that would never be me. That pain, that loss. Plus the fact that she would have to work with Amos daily.

Just like I worked with Ridge.

But I wasn't going to think about that.

I helped comfort a woman who needed it, and when Alexis took her back to her room, I gathered my things and headed off property. I didn't text Ridge where I was going. He already knew. And watching Naomi fall apart like that made me want to take a step back. Maybe just breathe. I didn't know.

I put my purse over my shoulder, grocery list in hand, and got out of the car to head into the store. I was tired and glad that I had mostly water that night and just half a glass of wine. I needed to get my head on straight, and that meant focusing on the task at hand and trying not to worry too much about Ridge.

"Aurora Lee?" an unfamiliar voice said from behind me, and the hair on the back of my neck stood on end as I turned.

I didn't know who it was, nor did I realize what was

happening until a large hand ripped the purse off my shoulder and two dots of pain hit my back. My knees went weak and I hit the ground, electricity shooting through my body as I realized that someone had hit me with a damn taser, stealing my purse.

I tried to scream but no words came out.

"Tell Ridge, remember." And then the man kicked me in the hip, a nauseating pain running through my body, and the electricity kept going until there was nothing, only darkness, only pain.

CHAPTER FOURTEEN

RIDGE

"I'm not playing tight end."

Brooks looked at me and shook his head. "But you're a great tight end."

"No, I'm a running back. You're the big one, you move just as fast, you're the tight end."

"Fine. But then who's going to be quarterback?"

"We've already established that I'm quarterback," Wyatt added.

"Do I get to play wide receiver then?" Elliot asked, and I rolled my eyes as we moved back.

"Yes. But try to catch the ball this time."

"I caught the ball last time, what are you talking about."

"It's okay, Ellie, we all know you can't . . ." Grace said from the other side of the field, and I huffed.

"Stop calling him . . ."

ball," East growled. "That means you're probably going to go easy on him."

"Hey, you're on my team," Elliot argued, and I laughed, taking a step back.

We were playing five-on-five, which I thought was amazing considering we were just doing it with the blood relatives. When Eliza hung out with us, the only Wilder cousin that wasn't a dude, she would play on both sides, and was probably the best punter we had. Except for that one time when we used two trees for a field goal and she ended up breaking a window. She could run faster than any of us when we were in trouble. I couldn't help but remember those times when we had all been dirty and had bruised knees and knuckles from wrestling and being dorks. And then when Eliza had wanted us to play 'girl games'—her words—we had all joined in, and I'd even gotten a makeover or two. Not that I would let anyone else know that. But we'd all done it together. And now here we were, doing it again. The whole damn reason we had moved here.

"Okay, let's get this done."

We moved into formation, and since we weren't using a center, Wyatt snapped the ball himself.

I moved to my position, since we were doing a passing play, and ran into Eli, who was wide, tall, and nearly knocked the breath out of me. Considering how hard I trained every day to do my job, it was a little disconcerting that a man who sat behind a desk all day could kick my ass.

He just smirked at me, and I scowled up at him.

"Excuse me, I thought we were playing flag football."

"Touch football, dumbass. Here let me help you up." Eli lifted me up to my feet in one quick movement, and I shook my head.

"What do you lift?"

"Wouldn't you like to know?"

"Did you put a whole gym in your house?"

"Much to Alexis's consternation, but then, she likes my muscles, so why not?"

I shoved at his shoulder as I laughed and we got back into position.

We were up by seven when Trace's phone rang, and since it was the emergency ping, we all stopped so he could answer. I went to get my water, my gaze on him when he turned to me and scowled.

"I got it. We're on our way."

I set down my drink and made my way over to him. "What is it?"

"She's fine. She's okay."

Those words were like a splash of ice water over me,

and bile filled my mouth as I forced myself to take deep breaths so I wouldn't pass out.

It was happening all over again. As soon as I started to care for someone, they needed me and I wasn't there. I wasn't strong enough. I couldn't protect them.

Something had happened to Aurora. I knew it. And I hadn't been there to protect her.

I didn't want to hear him say that. I couldn't.

Because all I could do was hear the doctors tell Heather's parents that she was dead. That our baby was dead.

I could still see her lying in my arms, blood pooling over her stomach and her thighs as I tried to stanch the bleeding. She had put her hands over her flat stomach, trying to protect the baby, and I had done the same thing, only I hadn't been strong enough. Blood had seeped through the glass shards in my arm and from the graze over my thigh where the bullet had struck. I had nearly forgotten that. The pain searing into my body when the bullets were fired. The people with a hate in their heart and eyes and bodies had come for us, all because we were out there enjoying life, supporting everyone at a homecoming parade for the cheerleaders.

And because our lives weren't exactly what people wanted them to be, they had shot into the stands and crowds. I had forgotten about the glass in my skin as I had shouted for help. But when it came, it had been too late.

I couldn't be too late again. I couldn't.

Trace put his hand on my shoulder, pulling me out of my memories.

"Ridge, Aurora's fine. She was seemingly mugged in front of the grocery store on her way home. She's at the hospital now. They took her purse and wallet and phone and everything, so she was able to get them to call here to let us know what had happened once she got settled. My team got the news to me. Because we're not family or her emergency contact, we're not allowed to know anything more than that. They literally cannot tell us what's going on medically, but we do know that she's okay because that is what she told them to tell us. So we are going to head to the hospital now to go see her. I need you to breathe. You're so fucking pale right now I have no idea if you're even listening to me. Can you hear me? I need you to say something."

"I'll call the girls," Eli said from my side, and that's when I realized that my brothers and cousins had all come to surround me, and I saw Wyatt on the phone beside me. He had to be calling Gabriel. Because that's what our family did, we came together. Now, anyway, we did. Not so much before, but we were figuring it out now.

"I'm fine." I coughed, clearing my throat. "I'm fine. I'll go see her."

"You're not fucking driving," Trace ordered.

"You already told me you weren't my boss; we've discussed this. I'm driving."

"We can take your car, but I'm driving you there. One of my guys or one of these Wilders can follow in another car. But you don't get to go alone."

"Damn straight," Alexis said as she stomped towards us. "We were just with her. She's one of us now. She's been initiated into the girls' club, and if my friend is hurt, I want to see her."

I ran my hands over my face, needing to get out of there. But I was seriously afraid of seeing Aurora injured in any state. And that was wrong. That was on me and I needed to fix it.

"I don't fucking care. I just need to go."

I knew I was being an asshole, but Aurora was alone. Alone and hurt. How the hell had someone mugged her in broad daylight? It was still light enough at seven o'clock in the evening that someone had to have seen something.

I jumped in my SUV with Trace driving. I didn't care in the moment to fight about who was driving, I just needed to get there. Wyatt and Brooks jumped in the back, and I knew there were at least two more SUVs behind us.

"Not all of us are going to be able to get into the back to see her. Hospitals are careful about things like that," Brooks said.

Brooks had dealt with hospitals enough that he knew. Of course, he knew.

"Are you sure you're up for this?" I asked, my voice hollow.

"Just like you are, brother. We've got you. And when it needs to be just the two of you, we'll make sure that happens."

"And we did the math so there's enough space in the other SUVs for the three of us to head back in it, and maybe go pick up Aurora's car."

"You don't have the keys," Brooks put in.

"Alexis said she has a keypad on her front door and she changes the number frequently, so one of us can get in and get her spare car key. Or whatever needs to be done. We'll handle it. You just worry about Aurora; we'll worry about the details."

Part of me relaxed, while the rest of me panicked, needing to see her. It felt like it took hours to get there, but it only took about forty minutes. Which, thanks to traffic in South Texas, really wasn't that bad.

But all I could do was keep hearing Heather scream,

hearing her family push me out of the hospital waiting area as they screamed at me. I could still feel her father's fists on my face from when he hit me. It hadn't mattered that I had been bleeding too, that I hid my own bullet wound just so I could see her. The doctors had stitched me up, and when I explained about the baby, I had finally been able to get news. The day had never made sense, and yet I could still hear it all repeating, hear the screaming over and over.

But this wasn't then. Aurora would be fine.

And yet, deep down inside, I wasn't sure that was the case.

She was not Heather. She was not the woman that I had loved and who had been carrying my child.

They kept talking, and I knew they would handle the details, but I needed to get there. We finally pulled in and I jumped out of the car when Trace finally stopped.

I made my way in, and then realized once again I wasn't family. I had no right to be there. But Aurora's family was up north all in a different state. They couldn't come down here this quickly. Maybe her best friend Joni would be there. I had met her and her husband a couple of days ago for a quick dinner, and I didn't even have their number. And if Aurora didn't have her phone, we were all fucked.

I knew my family would make their way into the waiting room as well, and Trace would deal with my car, but I needed to see her.

I walked up to the front desk and swallowed hard as the nurse looked up at me.

"How can I help you?"

"I'm looking for Aurora Lee. She was brought in earlier. Someone called to let us know she was here because the muggers took her phone."

I wasn't sure what else to say. The woman looked at me and smiled. "Are you family?"

"No, I'm her boyfriend." That was the first time I had said it out loud, but it was the best label I could come up with, more efficient than saying I was the man she was sleeping with and dating.

"What's your name, son?" the woman asked, and I shook myself out of my own fucking head. "Ridge Wilder." She looked down at her paperwork and nodded. "Aurora put you down as someone that we're allowed to bring back. So come on. She's fine. She explicitly said that you were allowed to know what was going on. She seemed very adamant about that."

Relief settled into me as I staggered, holding onto the wall.

Of course, Aurora would be adamant about that. Because I had told her what happened with Heather and the baby. Of course, Aurora would be thinking of me when she had been mugged.

"Do you know what happened?"

"She's speaking with the police right now, but from what she said, someone said her name, tased her, stole her purse and phone, and then kicked her in the hip. She has some bruising and is going to be sore for quite a while but is fine. No permanent damage. Now, why don't you go talk to her because I see the cops are leaving."

I stood there, frozen in place as I tried to move forward, as I tried to tell myself that this was fine.

I couldn't go through this again. I couldn't lose her again.

No, that wasn't right. I had lost Heather. I hadn't lost Aurora. They weren't the same person.

I couldn't do this.

But then I was moving, because she couldn't be alone, and I could feel the nurse's gaze on me.

I must have said thank you because she said you're welcome, and then I was inside the room, looking at Aurora, who looked so tiny in that large hospital bed.

There was a bruise on her chin, and her face was scraped up a bit where she must have fallen. I wanted to murder the man that hurt her.

"Ridge. I'm okay. I'm so glad that they called the Wilders for me. I couldn't remember anyone's phone number. That is so stupid, right? I used to remember every single phone number, now that we have cell phones I don't remember anything." She was babbling, and I knew she was scared but was trying to calm me down.

How fucking selfish was I?

I crossed the room so I was standing next to her bed and cupped her unharmed cheek.

"Are you really okay?"

Tears filled her eyes and she blinked them away.

I would kill the man who had caused those tears.

"I'm fine. I promise. I don't know what happened. It was a little scary. I don't know how the man knew my name."

That worried me, but I set it aside as something I would talk with Trace about. He had friends in the local sheriff's office so maybe they would know more about what had happened. Because that was an anomaly. Someone who mugged you didn't typically know your name.

"We'll figure it out. Between Trace and me and the cops, we'll find out who did this."

"They took all my things. It's going to take forever to get all those cards and everything replaced."

"Get Elliot on it. Between him and Alexis, they'll get it done in a couple of days."

I wasn't joking, and from the way that she smiled, she knew it.

"That is true. I just hate annoying people and taking their time."

"Don't be. Alexis said you were one of them. So you've been assimilated into the Wilder friends and family." I winced. "I'm not good at this, Aurora. I'm just glad you're okay."

She frowned. "I'm sorry you had to come out here."

"It's okay. As long as you're fine, we'll figure things out."

"We've got a code blue."

More words came over the intercom and I froze, Aurora's hand tightening on mine.

This was happening all over again. Aurora was bruised, hurt, and had been alone.

I couldn't do this. My chest seized, and I felt like I was gasping for air.

"Trace is going to be here in a minute, and he and Alexis will make sure you have what you need so you can get home and rest."

She frowned, confused.

"What's wrong?" she asked, her voice breaking.

"I just, I know this is going to be a lot for you. I don't

want to be in the way. So I'm going to give you some space."

I heard the words coming out of my mouth, and knew they were idiotic and a copout. But I couldn't stop them.

There was nothing more for me to say.

"I'm really fine. Yes, I'm a little sore, but you don't need to go."

Someone shouted in the ER behind us, a baby cried, and all I could hear were the sirens and the screams of the dying.

It was as if a switch had gone off, and Aurora seemed to understand. Her hand fell from mine.

"Oh. Right. I'll make sure Trace and Alexis are allowed to come back. And I'll let Kendall know that my iPad is in the office, and that it has all my contacts and things. You know, the cloud and all that. Don't worry about me. I'm really okay. Why don't you go get some air? I know this has to be a lot for you."

She kept speaking, but I couldn't hear her words. The only sensation I knew was pain.

Suddenly Elliot was there, and I remembered that he volunteered here during his free time, considering his previous job. I could feel the concern in his eyes when he looked at me, but then he was smiling at Aurora.

"Well, I guess you wanted to get out of inventory later. I see how it is."

Aurora smiled, but it didn't reach her eyes.

"I know, right? I can't help it. But don't worry, I can maybe help from a chair somewhere."

"No, you're going to be resting. We'll take care of you." I staggered off the bed and reached out to squeeze Aurora's leg to make sure that she knew I wasn't leaving forever, I just needed air. But she winced at the contact, and I realized it must've been one of her bruises, so I fell back and nearly landed on Trace. I didn't know how he was back here too, but maybe he was on a list somewhere. Maybe my mind wasn't clicking correctly.

"Why don't I take Ridge out for some air, and we'll be right back, okay?"

The worry on Aurora's face made me want to scream, made me want to hide.

But when I looked at her, I just saw Heather, and I knew I was going to throw up if I didn't leave.

I didn't even know what was happening, but then Trace was pulling me through doors and hallways that I couldn't pay attention to, and then my hands were on my knees as I retched into a bush, memories assaulting me one after another.

"There you go. Get it out."

"Fuck."

"I get it. You're okay. She's not going to blame you."

"I'm going to blame myself."

"She knows what's going through your head right now, we all do. Just breathe, okay? Then we'll get back in there."

"No, I can't go back in there. I'll just, I'll see her, I'll see her soon. I just, I need to go or I'm going to break, and I thought I was stronger than this."

Trace pulled me up to meet my gaze and frowned.

"We'll take care of her. She's family now. But you are too, Ridge. Think about what you want. Because you're just going to hurt both you and her if this is too much."

"I didn't expect her."

A small smile played on his lips and he nodded. "We never expect them. But when they show up, they just knock you over and it takes every ounce of strength you have to keep standing. But it's worth it, you know. You're strong, Ridge. With all you went through? You're so damn strong. Remember that. But don't hurt her along the way as you're trying to remember how strong you can be."

"I saw Heather there, not Aurora. And I hate that because they are not the same. I don't even feel the same." I held up my hand. "That's something I need to talk about with Aurora once I get it through my head, but right now we need to focus on the fact that she was hurt, and whoever hurt her knew her name, Trace."

Trace's eyes narrowed.

"Tell me everything."

I shook my head. "That's all I know."

"Then we'll figure it out. And we'll keep her safe. But you need to breathe."

"I need to go back in. But I can't. I'll follow you guys home. But I can't walk in there."

Trace gave me a sad look and nodded before he pulled out his phone.

I knew choices had to be made.

I needed to get my act together.

Someone had hurt her; someone had known her name.

And I had already been too late twice.

I didn't think I'd get a third time.

CHAPTER FIFTEEN
AURORA

Going about your life after you'd been mugged and tased and hurt felt weird in so many ways. This was not something I'd ever planned for and I never thought I'd be here, in pain, working from home on designs and pretending that I only hurt on the outside.

Because that wasn't the case.

My heart ached just as much, if not more, than my physical injuries and I wasn't sure how to fix it, or even if I should go about trying to find a way to.

While we still didn't know who had taken my purse, who had hurt me, I knew the authorities, as well as Trace and the others, were doing all that they could to find them.

It was odd to have so many people care about me,

and I didn't even know where they had all come from. My parents loved me. They were there for me throughout my entire childhood and beyond. When I married William, we moved for his job—and mine, considering I worked with his family. That distance from my parents had made maintaining our relationship difficult, but not impossible. Because I was still with them in my heart. And I knew they would drop everything to come and take care of me if I needed them.

I hadn't really given them a choice this time. I hadn't wanted to hide this from them, but wanted to keep it close so they didn't worry about me. But I also knew they needed to know everything. Primarily because if that person could unlock my phone, they could contact my family. So I used my tablet and the cloud to sync my new phone and get everything situated and explain to people what happened. So far nothing had come from it. No weird charges on my cards, no calls, nothing to impact my identity.

My parents had wanted to fly down and wrap me in cotton wool and never let me out of their sight again; keeping them away had been difficult.

But they had done their best to make sure I was taken care of.

But even with my parents not here, I wasn't alone.

Kendall came over every day with Alexis, and the other girls took turns coming over to take care of me. But I was fine. Yes, my hip was bruised a bit, and I was sore where the taser prongs had stuck into me, but I was fine. I would be back in the bakery the following day, despite Kendall trying to push me out. One of her friends from Dallas had come down to help as an emergency baker with the few wedding cakes I hadn't been able to do because I was sore and had been told not to overdo it.

That had hurt my heart because I wanted to do everything myself, but the clients understood and had been so grateful to find out we had backup plans for their cakes and desserts.

I just never wanted to disappoint anyone.

The Wilders had been so kind, so welcoming.

And Ridge had been there too. He hadn't come back to the hospital, which had worried me. Not for myself, because I could handle anything. I had proven that to myself repeatedly. I could do anything.

But the fact that his heart hurt so much, he couldn't look at me in a hospital bed? That worried me.

I was finding a way to move on, to be who I needed to be to become the person who didn't have to rely on my in-laws anymore. I didn't have to rely on anyone but myself. I was making friends and kicking ass and making the best cakes possible. Everyone missed my desserts already, even though the person who replaced me for the past couple of days was doing wonderful and was very talented, they still missed me.

I was needed. I was wanted.

After so many years of people telling me that I was replaceable, and that they didn't need me, things were completely different for me now and it was a good feeling to be wanted and needed.

No matter what happened with Ridge and me, I was not going to leave my place at the Wilder retreat. I was not going to be kicked out of my place, like I had been by Lauren and the others.

Because I knew the Wilders would never do that to me.

Though it hurt my heart to think about it.

I had to come to terms with what I felt for Ridge. And that was going to be a problem because I desperately craved to know what he felt for me.

I didn't know what was going on with him. I didn't know what he wanted or how he was feeling.

Because he wouldn't tell me.

And that was a problem.

When he hadn't come back into my hospital room, I was crushed, part of me worried that this had all been too much. That maybe he didn't really want me that way, maybe I wasn't who he needed.

But I had to focus on myself for the moment, at least that's what I kept telling myself, and also Elliot had been taking care of me, as well as Alexis and Kendall, so I hadn't been alone for long. We waited for the doctors to give me the go ahead and then I was out of there and on my way home.

Ridge had been waiting for me there, which had nearly tripped me up, my heart doing double-time at seeing him on my doorstep. I had given the Wilders the code to my house, something they had immediately changed just in case, even though it hadn't been written down anywhere or in my phone. But the Wilders were security conscious, and they had a damn good reason for that.

I had fallen into Ridge's arms, not on purpose, it just happened. And he had pushed my hair back from my face and smiled at me. But I'd seen the worry and the hurt there.

I didn't know if that was for me or the wrenching past that ached. And that is what burnt deep inside.

For the first day, he didn't leave my side. He made sure that I had some soup and was resting on the couch or in bed, and probably had overdone the overprotective man routine. But Elliot had told me that he had called himself my boyfriend, which had made me do a little giggle inside, and then wonder how mature I was. But I had never been in this situation before. I had only ever dated William, and that had been such a natural progression of a relationship because of our ages and how things just turned out. We had literally fallen into each other in love. Ridge and I? I was so deeply afraid that I was falling head over heels in love with a man that was never going to be able to love me back.

Not that he wouldn't want to. Not that part of him was telling himself that he couldn't move on and find whatever he needed. No, it was the fact that he was still in pain. I was three years more into my grief than he was, but in the end, did that matter?

Everybody grieved in their own way. There was no timeline of grief, or steps you could take until you finally found yourself whole and healed and everything was fine and you would just forget what had happened. No. That was not how things worked. And it took everything within me not to hold him down and beg him to love me.

I wasn't even strong enough to tell him that I loved him first.

He needed to figure out what he wanted, and I desperately needed to do the same.

And that was on me.

I would never know what Ridge wanted, or how close he was to finding out what that was, unless I asked.

But I still wasn't ready because I was terrified of the answer. Terrified that I would be wrong or I wouldn't be good enough.

And that was the crux of the damn problem.

Because I hadn't been good enough when fate ripped William out of my life. I hadn't been good enough for some of the people who should have held me close to them. Who should have shared their grief with me, and I them. They had pushed me away and hurt me when I was already in pain and I had to deal with the outcome.

But I was stronger than that now. I always had been, only it had taken me far too long to realize that.

I had ignored my family and Joni when they told me repeatedly that I was good enough. That I would always be good enough.

I was falling in love with Ridge Wilder, and honestly was probably already there.

But I didn't know what he wanted.

And that was something I was going to have to figure out. Far sooner than later.

Only, I had no idea how to ask him. Or even if it was worth asking at all.

And I truly needed to get out of my head so I could focus on who I was, and not who he might need me to be.

I pushed thoughts of Ridge out of my mind, which was mostly a lie, and wasn't easy, but I did my best.

Then I did the one thing I could and made my way into the kitchen to work on some thank you cookies.

It felt like going back in time, only a few short weeks ago when this had been my place of business. When I had only this option left to me when it came to work.

I was still so grateful for my friends who had stayed with me after William's death, who had helped me start my business. They had ordered cookies, told their friends, shared them on social media, and it helped me stay afloat.

It hadn't been enough. Creativity wise, financially, and heart wise, it hadn't.

But now I was doing things the way I wanted to.

I decided to make café au lait cookies and caramel cream Texas shaped cookies in thanks for the Wilders taking care of me over the past few days when I was recuperating.

Once the first batch of cookies was finally cool enough, I began tracing my outline so I could flood with icing.

It was intricate work, but I loved it. And it really stretched my muscles enough so I knew that I was ready for whatever came next. I had to ensure that I could handle baking with Kendall because she relied on me.

Although she was officially moving over to the signature restaurant soon, and I would be joining her there for special occasions, they had hired a new chef for the Wilder retreat so Kendall could spend more time with her family.

I would miss working with her every day, but it wasn't like the woman was leaving anytime soon. She was still our boss.

I went back to work right as my phone rang, and I used my elbow to answer, seeing that smiling face on the photo that popped up on screen.

"Joni!"

"You sound chipper. I wish I was there."

"You are at Disney World with your family. I'm so glad that you did not end your trip early."

"I just cannot believe you got attacked during the eight days that we were on a vacation. A vacation that I've been planning for two years. You'd think you could try to be a little more cognizant of my time?"

I snorted, then went on to the next cookie.

"I'm sorry. Next time I get attacked, I'll make sure you're home for it."

"How about you not get attacked? Let's just make that a rule. No attacking."

"I'll do my best."

"Damn straight."

"Seriously though. You worried me. But you're feeling okay now?"

"Honestly a little sore, but otherwise I feel great. I'm making cookies."

"Are you working? Kendall told me you wouldn't be working."

I laughed at that. The two had become fast friends, and I had a feeling that Joni would be joining the Wilder cheese and wine spreads every once in a while.

"I'm making thank you cookies. I'll make you and your family a batch once you get back, so they're fresh."

"Have I ever told you that I loved you?"

"Every time we talk."

"Well, just so you know. I love you so fricking much. Now, when am I seeing Ridge again?" she asked, and I did my best not to wince even though she couldn't see me.

She didn't know all of Ridge's past, because it wasn't my place to say anything. She also didn't know he hadn't come back into the hospital room.

Because I didn't know what he felt about me, and I didn't know if he wanted to keep going. But I would figure it out.

I would have to tell my friend. Once we were in person, and I could get it all out.

"I'm seeing him tomorrow. Tonight is just me and my cookies, and I couldn't be happier."

"Somehow you made that sound dirty, and I don't mind it. Okay, I have to go. This was our small break before we hit Hollywood Studios."

"You are a machine."

"Don't I know it. But Orlando makes me happy. I don't know why. I blame it on the water."

"Or the whole drinking around the world thing at Epcot."

"That too. I love you."

"I love you too."

I went back to my cookies once we hung up, and had just finished one batch of icing while the other batch cooled when my phone rang again, not with a call, but from the camera feed.

I frowned and set everything down, washing my hands quickly before I looked at the security readout.

My blood went cold, ice forming in my veins as I saw Lauren on the screen.

Trace and Ridge had added a few extra cameras

around my house, making sure I was safe since the attacker had my home address. That made me feel ill, but for some reason not as ill as seeing Lauren standing there.

But I couldn't just make her stay out there, I had to go and fix this.

Or at least get this over with.

I made my way to the door, telling myself that I was fine. That she could judge all she wanted, she could hate me, but nothing she said would ever bring William back.

I finally opened the door and saw her standing there, her face pale, a small awkward smile etched on her features.

She had her hands in front of her, clasped together so tight I could see her knuckles turning white.

"I'm so glad you opened the door. I was a little afraid that you wouldn't."

I wasn't quite sure what to say to that. I wasn't sure I wanted to let her in either. But standing in front of the door open like this would defeat the whole security thing, so I cleared my throat and took a step back.

"Come on in."

"Thank you for this, really."

This didn't seem like the Lauren I knew. Had something possessed her? Maybe she got tased too and her brain had got all jumbled.

No, that wasn't kind. Lauren had always been uptight, but she hadn't been so hateful until William died. Grief did so many things to us, different complicated things that made it hard to breathe. But all of that still didn't give Lauren the right to treat me like she had.

"I just wanted to say I'm sorry."

I stared at her, confused, wondering what the hell was happening right now. I didn't have a chance to speak because she continued.

"You don't have to say anything. But I finally did the one thing I should have done five years ago. I went to a therapist." She threw her hands up in the air, then put them back in front of her, clenching them tight.

"Lauren, I'm glad you're talking to someone."

What else was I supposed to say?

"I lashed out at you so many times. Because it was easier to hate you than to hate God, or to hate fate, or just hate the fact that my brother was dead. It wasn't your fault. It was the fault of the drunk driver. I know that. Everyone knows that. But it took me so long to figure out. And you just kept taking so many lashes. You are an amazingly strong person who was grieving just like me, but I didn't see that. I'm sorry. I'm sorry for not only hurting you, but for pushing you out of our lives and the business. I don't even know how you kept afloat with me being such a bitch. And I have no way of making it better. But I'm here to say I'm sorry, and that I'll do better. I won't bother you again. I won't hurt you. I just wanted you to know."

"Lauren." I let out a breath, trying to make her words make sense.

Because nothing made sense right now.

"I'm sorry too."

"What on earth do you have to apologize for? I'm the raging bitch."

I laughed, soft and low. "Well, I didn't say it, you did."

She grinned then, and it felt like it used to. Like when we were close, when William was still alive. I'd nearly forgotten those times. But they were there.

"You lost your brother. And I know it's terrible. I still feel it. Even when I'm smiling and I'm really okay. I've had to learn to be okay if I want to keep breathing. To survive. So know that you are going to figure that out too. I promise. Thank you for saying you're sorry. What you did over the years was not okay, but I forgive you. Because that's what William would've wanted."

Lauren wiped away tears and frowned at me. "I'm pretty sure William would've called me a bitch and told me to stop acting like it. I don't think he would've forgiven me."

"Oh, he may have said that, but he loved you and would have forgiven you. Because you're his sister. And me hating you isn't going to bring him back and isn't going to make it better. All it's going to do is to remind me of what we both lost and make it harder for me to move on."

"Are you? Moving on?" She held up both hands. "I'm sorry. That's totally none of my business."

"It's not. And I don't know. At least not in the way you're thinking. But I'm moving on with who I am. And that's what matters. It should matter for you too. You need to figure out who you are now. Even if it hurts."

She smiled then, but I didn't reach out to hug her. She had never been physically demonstrative and never really liked hugs. But we smiled and spoke a few minutes more. And then I said goodbye, waving at her as she left. I let out a breath; I hadn't been expecting that. But she had been a bigger person. Finally. And she had found her strength.

I would have to find mine.

Somehow.

CHAPTER SIXTEEN
AURORA

Yesterday had been an oddly emotional and yet uplifting day. It wasn't what I had been expecting, but it was something.

I hummed to myself as I worked, focusing on the cake in front of me. It felt amazing to be back at work, as if this was what I had been missing this whole time.

I needed to be elbow-deep in frosting, and any other sweet ingredient I could get my hands on, and just enjoy myself.

Everywhere I looked, though, somebody was trying to make sure that I took care of myself.

Nearly everybody had taken time out of their day to try and help me with things, whether it was making sure that I was hydrated, eating enough, or not lifting things that they thought were too heavy. Kendall's husband had even wordlessly found me a comfortable bouncy stool so I wouldn't have to stand all day bent over while working on florets. He hadn't said a word. In fact, he had scowled, growled something that I wasn't quite sure was even a word, and then went away after kissing his wife hard on the mouth.

I had raised both brows at her, but she just looked dreamy. The fact that they had been married that long and could still be dreamy like that? That was relationship goals.

My stomach ached at that because I wanted those relationship goals. I wanted that happiness.

Which was odd because I had just been thinking that I didn't. That it was too much for me, that I didn't need anything like that.

But here I was, changing my mind.

Because I wanted Ridge Wilder.

My sister-in-law coming to me, ready to change who she was because of the pain she was in, made me realize that I deserved it too. I deserved happiness, even though I was so afraid to take that step.

And if it wasn't with Ridge, I needed to know sooner rather than later.

And wasn't that a scary thought.

"Those rosettes are coming out fantastic." I turned to Naomi and smiled. The innkeeper had dark circles under her eyes, as if she hadn't been sleeping, and I didn't want to pry. Of course, she worked long hours for the Wilders and was always on hand if any of the guests needed her. She worked so hard as the innkeeper, and I knew the Wilders paid her well for it, but I wasn't sure how working with Amos might be affecting her mental health. Only, I didn't know her well enough to ask. It wasn't my place. Maybe one day, but when that day came, hopefully she would be in a better place.

"Thank you. I'm trying really hard."

"I can tell. Seriously, they look great. And I know you're busy, but I have a request."

I looked up from what I was doing and smiled. "Hit me."

"LJ's birthday is coming up. He is a friend of the Wilders." She came closer, a smile on her face. "He is, I promise. It's a very long story of how he's connected to the family, and him and his new wife are adorable. But, he keeps saying he doesn't want to celebrate his birthday."

"Which is a lot of crap," Kendall put in as she walked into the kitchen. I was so happy to see her that I nearly dropped the piping bag.

Instead, I just smiled. "You're here."

"I am. I'm not working until tonight, but everything was going well so I figured I'd come back since I was only here earlier to make sure you didn't overdo it. We're doing good, Chef?"

Chef Isaac nodded and went back to dicing a lot of vegetables. He was a quiet chef, but everyone else was allowed to be as loud as they wanted. We had a good rapport so far, and I enjoyed working beside him. Plus, he made some amazing food.

"Anyway, my office is still here, so I thought I'd come and say hi. And make sure that you're not lifting too much."

"I promise. None of the Wilders will let me."

"It was in the staff memo to make sure that you didn't." Naomi winked and I sighed.

"Are you kidding me?"

"Sadly not. But we care about you. We want you safe."

"Well, thank you. I really am okay. A little bruised, but those will heal. And I could have come in yesterday or even the day before. I missed seeing you guys and working."

"You had your sketchbook at home and we had online meetings with clients. You're doing great. Now, have you taken a break?"

"Your husband came in and made sure I was resting on this chair. I promise I'm doing great."

"He really is the best, isn't he?"

Once again, that dreamy look came over her face, and Naomi and I met gazes. Something sad crossed over hers, and I hoped that wasn't my expression as well. I just wanted Ridge to figure out what he wanted. Of course, I should probably ask him to get the answer. I needed to communicate the one thing I had realized that I hated. So I was going to fix that. Somehow. Even if it kicked my ass.

"Anyway," I said after a moment looking back at Naomi, "so he doesn't want anything for his birthday, but you're asking for something from me for his birthday?" I asked, slightly confused.

Kendall just laughed and waved on her way to the office.

"Yes," Naomi answered. "Pretty much. Can you make a cake? We'll totally bill it to the Wilders' tab." She laughed. "But with their permission, I promise. But he's our lawyer and does so much for us. And well, I guess we're a family."

My heart swelled. I loved working with these people. Even if someone didn't have the last name Wilder, they brought you in and made sure you were safe and loved and happy. I wouldn't want to be anywhere else. No matter what happened with Ridge.

"What is it you're looking for?"

"He is a coffee addict. But he also likes cream and

sugar in his coffee, and whipped cream and caramel sauce if nobody's looking." She winked. "I'm the innkeeper. I'm supposed to notice little things like that."

I laughed and took notes. "So, how many people are we feeding?"

"Well, he has a meeting coming up on his birthday here. So enough for the staff, which is over a hundred people at this point, which is insane when I think back to how many were here at the start."

I shook my head. "We can do that. Plus leftovers for anyone to take home, including LJ. Will his wife be here?"

"Yes, because she's in on it. She cannot bake, so she's asking for help."

I laughed at that. "Well, I'm your girl. So, we want sort of a sweet latte coffee cake, but not actual coffee cake," I corrected, as Naomi frowned.

"Yes, not crumbly. Something soft and airy with tons of buttercream frosting. He's a buttercream frosting guy."

"That was my next question. I could have fun with that. And now I'm thinking about shapes and every-thing, and I might also make some cupcakes."

"Really?"

"Cupcakes are fun, and can help me with the

design. Oh, this is going to be great. And I'll make sure that the company knows what supplies I need, but I'm not charging for this. If you say that LJ is part of the family, and you say that I am as well, that means I'm doing this for family."

"You are the best."

I smiled wide as I finished taking notes and Naomi went back to work. I set my notebook aside and went back to florets. When it was time for me to lift the next tier, I rolled my shoulders back. I was still sore, but I could handle it.

"Here, let me help."

I nearly fumbled the layer at the sound of that deep voice. That deep voice just did things to me.

Why was he like this? Why did he do this to me without even trying?

But no, that wasn't his fault. That was on me. My need for him, my need to change what I had once craved.

He put his hands on my shoulders, keeping me steady as I held onto the cake.

"Let me take that from you."

"I got it." I hadn't meant the words to come out so sharp, and when he turned to look at me, he frowned.

"I'm sorry, I didn't mean to startle you. I promise."

"I'm really okay. Let me just set this and then I'll be

all yours." I paused. "Or for whatever you need. For work. Or you know. I'm rambling."

I couldn't read the expression on his face. I wanted to know what that expression meant. I had been getting close to figuring out his tells and what he was feeling. But then he closed himself off after the hospital. And I couldn't handle that. Not when I had a great love with open communication once.

I wasn't saying I was comparing the two of them. That wouldn't be fair to either William or Ridge. But knowing my worth in these situations, that's what I could compare. And I would. Even as it broke me.

"I just wanted to see if you could take a little break. I won't take you away for long. I promise."

There was such an earnest look to him now, and *that* I could read. I didn't want him to break up with me right now, to say that it was too much and he couldn't handle it. Just the thought of that made my stomach ache, but he wouldn't do that. Not right now. Not in the middle of work where everything was just so complicated and convoluted. No, he was better than that.

No matter what happened, no matter how hurt he may be, no matter how far in the past he was, he was better than that. I needed to get my head out of the clouds, or the sand, and remember that.

We were both better than that.

"Okay. Just let me set this." He stood back as I set the final tier on the dowels. Because the cake was so large, I had wanted to get the bottom layers fully decorated before I added the top layer. One time I had accidentally leaned into a cake while decorating the top and it had turned into a whole disaster, and I wasn't looking to repeat that experience. When I stepped back, the dark chocolate decadent monstrosity in front of me shone underneath the lights.

"Now, that is fully decadent."

"I just want to smash my face into it and eat it all."

I turned, arms outstretched as I blocked him from getting to the cake. "If you try that, I will knee you in the nuts. And I have bony knees."

"I know you have bony knees. Because you did accidentally knee me that one time." His voice went low at that, and I blushed all the way to the tips of my ears.

"Ridge."

"I'm just saying. Seriously though, that looks so delicious my mouth is watering."

"Thank you." I blushed again, this time under his praise. "I need to get it into the refrigerator so it sets and then I can talk." I took a slow breath. "Will you help?"

His shoulders sagged in relief at my question, and I

knew it had been the right thing to say, even though I had no idea what would come next.

"Just tell me what to do. I'm all yours."

I blushed again, even though there was no reason for it. As everyone watched, we made our way around the table and each took a side of the stand and set it on the cart. It was easier to wheel, because I wasn't one of those people who could lift an entire cake on my own and carry it into the cooler. There was a reason we had the system set up the way we did. Once I locked the cake in the fridge, I sent my notes so everyone knew where things were since the team that worked under me and Chef Isaac would need to know where everything was so they could do their jobs.

Then I followed Ridge out of the kitchen and into the small courtyard. It was cold enough that there were very few flowers, just the small winter ones that seemed to thrive in the lack of heat. It wasn't too cold though, and I was still warm from work, and so I sat down on one of the stone benches and lifted my face up to the sun. "I don't know why that feels so good. Probably because I've been bent over cake all day."

"And you're allowed to? You've been cleared for working like that?"

I heard the worry in his voice, and I instinctively reached out to squeeze his hand in reassurance. "Yes.

I've been all cleared, though nobody would let me back to work until today."

"I saw the memos."

I looked at him and grimaced. "I thought Naomi was just joking."

"No, Alexis and Kendall and Maddie are determined. But don't worry, you're taken care of."

"I know."

He reached out and pushed my hair back from my face, and I let out a small worried breath.

"I'm sorry."

I swallowed hard. "For what?" I wasn't playing dense. There were so many things he could be referring to, and yet so many things that he shouldn't be sorry for.

"I'm an idiot."

My lips twitched. "That doesn't explain much, Ridge. Not to be mean."

"Thankfully." He smiled with me and tweaked my nose. It was such a sweet gesture that I laughed, and his shoulders relaxed at the sound. This felt normal. Like it should be. I just needed us to stay that way.

"When I looked at you in that hospital bed, I saw Heather. I wasn't prepared for that."

I swallowed hard and nodded. "I figured it was

something like that." The hollow ache within me started to gain ground, but he squeezed my hand.

"I don't see Heather when I see you. I loved Heather. I was *in* love with her. But just like you with William, we aren't those people anymore."

I nodded, my throat tightening. "I know. I'm not the woman that William loved."

"I couldn't protect Heather. And that was the trigger, seeing you there. Not that it was you in the hospital bed. Not that it wasn't her. It was that I couldn't protect you."

"You weren't even there."

"That doesn't mean anything to my memories of that moment. Part of me thought I could keep you safe by keeping you away, and that was the most idiotic thing I could have done."

I shook my head. "Maybe not most idiotic, but it's up there, Ridge. You being there had nothing to do with what happened."

"Maybe not. But, I don't know, maybe if I'd been standing there, the guy wouldn't have come at you. Whoever it was. Because he knew your name. He called you by your name. And we don't know why he knew that or why he targeted you."

Ice settled over me again, but I swallowed it back. "I know. I have to hope that he just knew me from work, or my old job and thought I'd be someone easy to rob. And it ended up being fairly easy for him."

"I still don't like that. It's so unnerving."

I nodded. "Same. But you and Trace have done your best to keep my house safe, and I know I'm safe here because all of you work so hard to keep your families and your people safe. That's not something that you can handle by yourself. Not all of the responsibility of the world is on your shoulders. But you can't push me away when things get tough, or you get scared. Because I spent years watching people push me away when they didn't want to think about what was lost. And I can't go through that again."

I let out a breath as he nodded. "Because I care about you."

I needed to say the words for me. Not for him. And if he said this was too much and walked away, then I would understand. I would hate it and it would break my heart for a while, but I had learned to put myself back together once and I could do it again. But the only way I could even begin to accomplish that was by making sure he knew what I felt. I didn't know if I could let myself love him. Because of that fear. But I could let him know a little part. As much as I could for now.

"I care about you too." He pushed my hair back from my face again and cupped my cheek. "I'm so damn sorry. I never want to put my past or yours over our present. That's my promise to you. I'm going to do better. I'm not going to be that asshole."

"Thank you." I blushed. "I'm not sure what I was supposed to say to that. Other than I'm going to try too." He laughed then, the most joyous sound in the world, and leaned down to take my lips with his.

And in that moment, I knew we would be okay. Because this was a step. Maybe not the biggest step. But it was a step in the right direction.

I was the new me. And Ridge could be mine. As long as I took that next step, and he did too.

By the end of the day, I was tired but still exhilarated. I was nearly home, alone in my car, despite Ridge wanting to be with me. But there had been another trespasser at the edge of the property who wanted to see Lark Thornbird again. I didn't know why people kept thinking they could do that, but they were getting bolder, which meant that Trace and Ridge had to work more.

And while I knew Ridge wanted to be with me, my house was safe because we had the security up. I would pull into my garage and not get out of my car until it was closed. I knew the rules, and I followed them to a T. I didn't want to get hurt again. Nor did I want to scare Ridge.

The fact that those thoughts went hand-in-hand should worry me, but then again, there was a reason he was the way he was. And he was trying. Just like I was. And that was a promise between us.

I pulled into my garage, did exactly what I was supposed to do, and headed inside. I was humming under my breath when a hand slid over my mouth, and I froze.

"Drop your phone, your purse. If you scream, I'll kill you. Just like I should have killed you before."

I knew that voice, I had heard that voice in my nightmares when he called my name. But I didn't know this man. I didn't know who that voice belonged to.

He squeezed my arm and pushed me down to the ground, but I didn't scream. I saw the gun and I knew he could kill me.

Instead, I just looked up into a face that was oddly familiar.

And then I knew.

This was the third man. I'd seen an article after I had looked it up when Ridge told me the story. I had remembered seeing something about it when it first happened, but now it was all very clear.

"Call Ridge. Call your little bitch boyfriend. We need to talk."

This was one of the men that had killed Ridge's girlfriend, who had killed so many people.

And one of the men Ridge had identified because he had seen him. And because he was so good at his job, he had remembered the details of their faces even after all that trauma.

Two were behind bars.

But this was the third man.

And I knew I wasn't getting out of here alive.

CHAPTER SEVENTEEN

RIDGE

"Do you have her all situated?" I asked, running my hand through my hair. I was so fucking annoyed. I had a million places to be and none of them was where I was now. I just wanted to get out of here and get to Aurora's. I hated that she lived so far away. Why the hell couldn't she just live closer? Why couldn't she just live here? Maybe even with me. It just made more sense for things to work out that way. That way we wouldn't spend so much time fucking traveling. We both worked long hours, and we both worked on this property. There were plenty of places for her to stay around the retreat that weren't even on property. We could probably find something. Something we could afford that wasn't too much to handle since we weren't home a lot. I bet we could find something.

I frowned, pausing mid thought when I realized I kept saying "we." *We* would find something. *We* would make things work.

As if there was a true future. As if I wanted her for more than just this moment.

But I did, didn't I? I had said care instead of love earlier because I had copped out, but I knew this feeling. I had felt it before, even though it had been a little different. But I knew that feeling.

That intense heat and churning and connection that came with knowing that person fit you perfectly.

And I had ignored it because I had been so damn scared. But what if it was okay to lean into that fear, to lean into being scared? What if it's okay?

Oh dear God, I loved Aurora Lee. I loved that damn beautiful cake maker who made me smile. Who made me believe.

How the hell had that happened? How had I gone from hiding within my own family and moving across the state so I wouldn't have to deal with anything connected to my past or feelings, to wanting her to be closer. For wanting us to be so close we practically lived together, or actually wanting to live together. How the hell had that happen?

"Ridge? Are you listening to a word I'm saying? What is going on in your head right now?"

I looked up at Trace who frowned at me, and I swallowed hard, running my hands over my face. "What? What did you say? What did I miss?"

"First, your voice is going really high-pitched, and I can see your heart beating with that flutter on your neck. So, breathe in and out, calm yourself, and slow down that pulse rate for me."

I did as he asked, mostly because I needed to do something other than have that quick panic attack in my head over and over and over again.

"Sorry. What did I ask?"

Trace gave me an odd look, and I realized I had possibly lost my mind.

"You asked if I could handle her. The obsessed fan who really wanted to get to know Lark and her husband. Yes, I can handle this. Why don't you go see Aurora, because I have a feeling whatever the hell is going on in that head of yours is something about her, and maybe something you want to tell her?"

"How the hell do you know that?" I asked, confused as hell.

"You have the same look that I had when I realized that I was fucking things up with Elliot and Sidney. I've got this, thanks for the help since two of our men are down with the flu. I appreciate it. Now, go see your girl. I like the two of you together."

"Really?" I asked with a snort.

"Yes. You two fit. She's so bubbly and happy when she lets herself be, and you need that."

"I don't like this whole intuitive side of you," I said dryly.

"Maybe not, but this is why we're friends. Go see my girl too and pick up some flowers."

I raised a brow. "Relationship advice?"

"I'll have you know I'm married to not one but two fucking fantastic people. If anyone is going to give you relationship advice out of every single person on this property, it's going to be me."

I laughed, shaking my head. "Well, I guess the odds are in your favor."

"May they ever be," he said with a laugh, and I ignored him, before taking his advice and going to Sidney to pick up flowers. I was a flower kind of guy. But I didn't know what I was doing.

I had just realized that I was in love with Aurora. So maybe I should do something about that. Maybe I should figure out exactly what I was supposed to do. Tell her? Well, that would probably be a good thing. Or maybe I should keep apologizing for being such a fuck face. Yes, that seemed like the thing to start with.

Or maybe I should just see her. I smiled, my shoulders relaxing. Yes, I just wanted to see her.

When Sidney smiled up at me, her fingers covered in band-aids and her hair piled on the top of her head in the messiest bun I'd ever seen, I just laughed.

"You okay?"

"Huge rose delivery day. I love roses, but I hate thorns. I'm sure there's a nice poetic thing that I could say, and Elliot would probably be the best at it, but I'm not in the mood. I just want wine."

"We do work at a winery. You'll probably figure it out."

"Yes, but I try not to wine and snip." She held up the snippers, and I winced.

"That makes sense. I mean, look at your hands with thorns already."

"I know. And both Elliot and Trace are going to be pissed off at me."

"Speaking of Trace, it was his suggestion I come over here for flowers."

Sidney smiled so wide I was afraid her cheeks were going to burst. "Really? For Aurora? That's the sweetest thing. I'll whip you up a bouquet real quick."

"Nothing too fancy? I mean, she deals with cakes every day. I would say wildflowers, but we are out of season."

"Very true. But I have an idea. A couple of roses, but light ones, just blooming from the hothouse that we have. I have a few other things that I could add so it's colorful and fun. You guys need fun after everything that happened. I hope that's okay to say."

"It is. Thank you, Sidney."

"You're so welcome. I love Aurora. The two of you are adorable."

I just shook my head, a smile playing on my face. "That seems to be the consensus."

"Well, we have good taste." She handed me a bouquet full of bright yellow and purple and red and orange and yellow flowers. "Here you go."

"How did you do that so quickly?"

"My hands are numb at this point," she said with a laugh. "And I like you. And I love Aurora."

"I'm family. Shouldn't you love me?" I asked, noticing that I could say the L word quite easily now. Look at that.

"Shush. I love you too. But you get all squirmy when I say it, so I don't."

I moved around the counter and hugged Sidney close, keeping the flowers safe.

"You are such a bright light. Thank you for bringing Elliot back when I hadn't even realized that we'd lost him."

I said that softly, so soft I could hear Sidney's sniffs.

"That's the sweetest thing. The freaking sweetest thing. And now I'm crying and I'm going to be all puffy for my date with my men tonight. But seriously, how do you know how to say the right thing?"

I pulled away, flowers in hand, and shook my head. "I'm the worst person when it comes to saying the right thing. Just ask Aurora."

"But she fixed it. Because those aren't apology flowers, are they? Because if so, I should have used different colors."

I shook my head. "No, we're past that. Well, at least a step past that. So these aren't truly apology flowers, but somewhere close. In the vicinity. Maybe just some 'I'm thinking of you and I missed you' flowers." I winced. "I have no idea how to say things with flowers."

"Flowers have a language of their own. So you're right on that."

"And these say what I need them to say?"

"I think you being there says that too." She smiled brightly, wiping away her tears. "Now, go see your girl. And tell her that girls' night with lots of cheese and lots of wine is tomorrow."

"That means she's staying here, and I can get a nicely cheesed up woman. I like that."

"All the men love that. It is one of the perks." She winked, and I just laughed, heading out to my car with a spring in my step.

I was excited to see her. It was about time.

I was just getting into my car when Wyatt came up, a frown on his face.

"You okay?" I asked, eager to get to Aurora's.

"Yeah. Just dealing with bullshit."

"Still waiting on papers?" I asked, since Wyatt had finally told me some of why he was such an asshole sometimes.

"Yep. And I have to pay another lawyer fee. I really love this. Don't you?"

"Are you good for it?" I asked, hating talking about money.

"Yes. I am. Plus every time that I try to pay, our baby brother and all his millions decide to get in the way. It's really fucking annoying."

I pressed my lips together, knowing that if Gabriel wouldn't do it, the rest of us would. Because we needed to take care of each other. And it was about damn time we got our heads out of our asses and figured that out.

"If you need anything, let me know. I'm heading to Aurora's tonight, but tomorrow's girls' night with wine and cheese. So maybe during that we can sit down and hash it out?"

"Maybe. I don't know. It's just a shitty night. But I have to head to the bar anyway."

"Okay. But maybe talk to Brooks. If you're in this mood, Brooks will help."

"Brooks has his own moods," he grumbled before stomping away as he muttered under his breath.

I had no idea how to fix things for him, but maybe it was time I tried. My brothers were floundering, just like I was. But I was getting out of it. Finally. So it was time to pass the torch.

Once I figured out exactly how to explain to Aurora what I felt. With words and everything.

I got in my car, kept the flowers safe on the front seat, and got on the highway to make the trip to Aurora's. It was only forty minutes without traffic, and thankfully we were past the major rush hour. But with the construction, you just never knew.

I was about five minutes away when my phone rang, Aurora's name coming over the dash.

I smiled, hitting answer as soon as I could.

"Hey, babe. I'm almost there. Can't wait to see you."

"Ridge?"

Aurora's voice sounded stilted, so fucking scared, and my hands gripped the steering wheel, because I could tell something was wrong.

"Aurora? What's wrong?"

"Ridge, stay away." She shouted the last part, and then there was a sound of flesh meeting flesh as she screamed, and I sped up, going ninety in a seventy.

"Aurora!"

"So sorry. Aurora can't come to the phone right now. But I see you're on your way. That saves some trouble. Get here soon, Ridge Wilder. I'm going to kill another one of your girls. I so liked doing it the first time."

The phone clicked off and I slammed my fist into the steering wheel, going far too fast down the highway, and hoping to hell I didn't crash or get pulled over.

I pressed the talk button, my voice brittle. "Call Trace."

Calling Trace.

"Hey, what's up," Trace asked after a single ring.

"I know who it is. It's the third asshole. The one that they thought went to Mexico. He's here. He's in Aurora's house. He has her. Call the cops. Do something. I'm like two minutes away." I skidded off the highway, praying that I didn't flip my fucking car.

"What, slow down. What's going on?" Trace pulled the phone away from his mouth and called out a few things, and I heard Elliot over the line saying he called 911.

"The third guy. The one they never caught? We all

thought he was either dead or vanished. But he's not. He's the one who mugged her. Had her address. I don't know how he got in, but he found a way. And he has her."

"I'm on my way. But it's going to take me some time. We're calling the cops. Don't do anything stupid, Ridge."

"He has Aurora. I'm going in."

"Fuck. Don't die. Don't get Aurora killed. We'll be there soon."

"I know." I hung up, grateful that Trace had everybody's information so he could handle the authorities.

I needed to get to Aurora.

I skidded into the driveway, and I knew that anyone who saw me probably thought I was insane.

But I didn't care. I didn't know how that man had gotten in there, but if he had evaded the cops for this long, he could find a fucking way. And I had let her go in alone. Again. But I'd be damned if she got hurt again because of me. I hadn't been there before or now. Because all of this was my fault. Because I'd identified those men.

Fuck this. I wouldn't let her die. This would not happen again.

I got out of the car and made my way to the door, my hands shaking until I forced myself to remember my training. I needed to be calm. I needed to be the guy who trained for this.

"I see you. You better not be armed." I looked up at the camera and realized he could see me, and would be able to hear me over the mic.

"Don't you fucking hurt her."

"Too late, bro. You got my brothers put in jail. I'm going to take what's yours again. I had so much fun the first time."

"You said that already. But why don't you take me instead? Let her go. I'm the one who fucked you over. She doesn't deserve any of this."

"She's trying to crawl out from where I hogtied her under the table. She's so cute. We left the front door unlocked for you. I want to see your face in person when I kill her."

I wasn't armed, I didn't carry a gun. I had only been driving to Aurora's house to see the woman that I loved. And now this man was going to try to take everything from me again. But I'd be damned if I let that happened.

I held up both hands so he could see I was stupidly unarmed. I looked straight at the camera, knowing I'd kill this man if I had a chance. But I didn't care, so I walked slowly to the front door and then opened it, and I knew this was one of the most idiotic things I had done.

He could shoot me right in the face, and there wouldn't be a damn thing I could do about it.

But if I didn't go in there? He'd kill her. There was no doubt about it in my mind.

"Be quick about it, bro. Before I kill her. Because I will. You know I will."

I opened the door and took a step in.

There was some blood on the carpet, but only a little from where her nose had bled and her lip had split. But she was alive, her mouth clamped closed as she looked at me with wide eyes. He must have told her not to scream.

I wanted to tell her that this would be okay, that we'd fix this, but I couldn't.

Not until I got her out of here.

"I'm here. You can let her go now."

"I don't think so. I'm the one who holds all the cards here. You're such an idiot. You should have just stayed away and stayed safe. But no, you always try to rescue the girl. Couldn't do that before so you got my brothers put in jail, but now it's my turn to finish you."

"Do what you want to me, just let her go."

"Ridge, don't."

"What did I fucking say?" the man snapped as he turned the gun to her.

With his back to me I did the one thing I could do. I

moved. I was trained, and this man wasn't. His grip on the gun looked like he had learned it from watching movies, and no practical experience.

He whirled on me as I hit him and a shot rang out, going wide.

And then another, and another.

But the man hit the ground with me on top of him, and I slammed my fist into his face, and then again and again, using my other hand to squeeze his wrist, and moved my leg to kick the gun away once he finally dropped it.

Fire spread over my shoulder, and I realized that a bullet had grazed me, but it wasn't a direct hit so it was fine. I'd been here before, after all, but I'd be damned if it ended like it had before. Blood seeped down my shirt, Aurora was crying, and sirens rang in the distance, growing closer. But I kept punching as the man went unconscious, blood splattered over my chest, over my fist, and then Aurora was moving towards me, her hands and legs still tied.

I looked over at her and nearly passed out. Before I went to her, I made sure the man was tied up and down for the count, then I moved to the woman I loved. She was so pale, so scared, but the man hadn't covered her mouth. He wanted to hear her screams.

"Ridge, you came."

"I'll always come when you need me," I whispered.

And then I moved to untie her wrists and her ankles, knowing that the man was unconscious but alive.

I hadn't killed him. I wanted to. I wanted to take him from this life so he could never hurt another person that I loved.

But I wouldn't. Not in front of Aurora.

If she hadn't been here? That might be a different story.

But for now, I just held her in my lap and let her shake as the sirens got closer.

"I'm here. I've got you."

"I'm so sorry. I'm so sorry that I didn't know he was in the house."

"We'll figure it all out." I held her face and looked over her bloody nose and lip.

"Are you hurt anywhere else?"

She shook her head, leaning back on my chest. "No, he just slapped me. I'm okay. But you're bleeding. Oh my God, Ridge, you're bleeding."

"I'll be fine. It's just a flesh wound."

She scowled. "But the knight who said that eventually lost all his limbs."

"I'm fine, I promise. I love you so fucking much, Aurora. You just need to be okay." My heart raced and I did my best not to squeeze her too tight, or set her aside so I could kill the man beside us.

"I'm okay. And I love you too. So much."

"I'm never letting you out of my sight again. You're going to move in with me and you're never going to leave. You're going to be stitched to my side until the end of days. Because I'm never letting this happen again. Do you understand me?"

Her eyes widened before she laughed, and I couldn't believe that we were laughing in this situation. "Did you just say you love me and ask me to move in with you within like three breaths?"

"I didn't ask, I said it was happening. That's an order, a demand. So get over it."

She shook her head before she leaned over and kissed me, and I knew this was it. This was everything.

This was the woman that I loved.

She pulled back and winced, so I held her close and rested my forehead on hers. "Sorry. That's got to hurt your lip."

"I'm fine. And okay, I'll move in with you. Because I love you too, and I really hate the drive."

I laughed as the cops came in and asked for *Ridge Wilder*, and everything became chaotic again.

We tried to explain to authorities what had happened as Trace barreled in, who must have somehow driven like a bat out of hell to get to us so quickly, and I knew we would be okay.

Because this was the woman that I loved. The woman that was mine.

I hadn't been too late this time.

I hadn't been too late.

CHAPTER EIGHTEEN
RIDGE

"Hands on the wall. Keep them steady. Don't slip."

"That's a tall order for the shower with no rubber duckies on the floor to keep us safe."

My lips twitched as I slid my hands over her hips, feeling every curve, every touch. She was so damn soft, so perfect. And I was in trouble.

"We can invest in rubber duckies at our next house. Or maybe tomorrow here. I don't care. Can't really think with your naked ass pressed against my cock. As you well know."

She laughed, then wiggled her hips so she rubbed against my dick, and I closed my eyes, trying to count to ten so I wouldn't spurt all over her back.

"Minx."

"You know me. We're trying to save the environment here by showering together, and look at us, wasting all this water."

"Then I better be quick about it."

I slid my hands between her folds, and she moaned as she arched back into me.

"Lift your leg onto the edge right there. It's nonskid. I'll keep you safe."

"You know, shower sex always looks better in movies than it is in real life." Then she let out a large gasp as I slid balls deep into her in one thrust, and her knees began to shake. I kept her steady, and turned the water down a bit so we wouldn't drown ourselves.

"What were you saying?"

"Nothing. Nothing at all. Do continue."

I bit down on her shoulder gently before I began to move, my free hand sliding up and down her hips to cup her breasts. I pinched her nipples between my forefinger and thumb, and she sighed, pressing back into my hips.

"I feel so full."

"Good. Now hold on tight. We're not done."

And then I really began to move, both of us arching into one another, the water sliding in between us. When my own knees began to shake, I turned off the water completely and dropped us both onto the plush

rug in front of the open shower. I was really apprecia-
tive that this was one of the showers without a door or
a curtain, and yet somehow didn't get water
everywhere.

I kissed her again and tapped her hips.

"Ride me."

"On the bathroom floor? Aren't I going to hurt your
back?"

"The potential bruises would be worth it."

Her eyes darkened at that, and I knew we were both
thinking the same thing. The bruises had healed but we
still remembered the other ones that had been there
and how they'd gotten there.

She moved, pulling me out of the past, and I held
on, both of us arching into one another. When she
finally came, I followed, bringing her down so I could
capture her lips with mine. I pinched the side of her hip,
loving the way she moaned into my mouth, that slight
bit of pain increasing her orgasm.

"I love you."

She smiled against my lips as she moved back so we
could look into each other's eyes.

"I love you too. And I'll never get over hearing you
say that." She pushed my hair back from my face, then
slid her fingers through my beard. "And I really love
feeling you deep inside me. I never used to dirty talk

before. I guess it's just the Wilder way." She winked as she said it, and I arched my hips, loving the way that her eyes nearly rolled back at that. "Okay. I have cakes to bake and cookies to make. I really can't do that with you deep inside me."

"I don't know. I'm sure we could make it a thing."

"Maybe we'll play baker and the taster one day, but for now, I really do need to shower. Alone." She slapped my chest as I tried to sit up, and we both groaned when she slid off me.

Thankfully, I got to watch her shower, and I was pretty sure she took her time on her breasts and between her thighs. So I stroked myself off again, and laughed when she stepped over me, clucking her tongue.

"That recovery time. I'm very blessed."

She began to get ready, blow drying her hair and putting on clothes, and I quickly showered, marveling at the fact that we were getting ready together, and this was going to be our life. Things would change, where we lived and how we mixed our schedules, but this was it. This was the happy ever after I had never let myself have before.

I had never thought I would fall in love again, that I would be able to fall in love at all. But Aurora had proved that you could have second chances.

And I hoped to hell I proved the same to her.

We headed into work, and I was happy to be back on regular duty. The graze on my shoulder had healed quickly and would leave a scar next to the other one. I didn't want to take a chance on the third times a charm gambit where that was concerned, however. I still had PT, but because it was only a graze and hadn't gone through bone or muscle, that meant I had time to focus on getting everything set up at the property and making sure that I was in top shape.

"Running late, are you?"

I looked at Trace who just smirked.

"Is that a hickey on your neck? I'm pretty sure you just got here too."

Trace flipped me off, and we looked over at the schedule boards.

"We've got a shit ton to do this week, so I'm glad you're back up on the schedule."

"Well, I'll try not to get shot again."

Trace glared at me. "You better not. I never want to see you bandaged and pale like that again. Scared the shit out of all of us."

"I promise, boss. I won't."

"Stop calling me boss. We both know that we share this position. You're a fucking Wilder, just like me."

I smirked. "Look at you. Being assimilated into the family."

"It's called being married in the family. But hell, I'm glad you're back full-time. Are you coming to the dinner?"

I shuddered. "Yes. Though I don't know how we're all going to fit in one house."

"That's why we're having it here. Don't worry, we have it all figured out. And make sure you bring Aurora."

"Of course I'm going to bring Aurora. Why wouldn't I?"

"That's what we like to hear. I'm really fucking glad someone stole that wedding dress."

I laughed outright, though we both looked over our shoulders just in case Alexis showed up.

"You're really glad that she didn't hear you say that."

"Tell me about it. She'd kill us both."

"And we'd deserve it."

Trace and I got to work, and then we headed out on a normal day. We had a small afternoon wedding, a high tea, a retirement party, and a few drunk tourists at the winery. The distillery was up and running, with Wyatt's assistant manager handling it, and everyone else moved about like a well-oiled machine.

It was odd to think that the Wilders had started out spread all over the world, trying to find a way to call themselves family. And now here we all were, making this place our own.

By the time we got off shift and I headed towards the restaurant to meet up with everyone, I was tired, but still exhilarated. Apparently morning sex was the way to start off the day. That was something I was going to put on the agenda, and hopefully Aurora would be on board with it.

As soon as I thought her name, she came through the door, and I smiled, opening my arms for her. She ran into them, and I laughed when she let out a shocked gasp and moved back.

"Did I hurt your shoulder?"

"I'm all healed, babe. Plus I think what we did this morning and last night would probably have hurt my shoulder more." She blushed as Gabriel laughed from behind her, and I flipped my brother off before I kissed Aurora hard on the mouth, then making our way into the dining area.

Kendall and her team had done all of the cooking, and I could spot Aurora's desserts everywhere. But everything was set up for family style, meaning we would feed ourselves, enjoy ourselves, and it would just be casual. Though, we did take up most of the space now.

Eli and Alexis were in the corner, laughing with Kylie as she giggled and ran around with Reese and Cassie, her cousins. Alexis looked a little green at the gills yet, and I knew soon there would be a new Wilder baby, probably with more following soon.

Evan and Kendall were over by the food, both of them laughing at each other, and then growling a bit. I loved their dynamic, and figured if it worked for them it could work for anyone.

Bethany and Lark sat at a small table, wine in hand as they laughed at something as Maddie walked up to them. When their men, Everett, East, and Elijah, came forward, the three men took their seats and everybody talked with and over one another, with wine being poured and cheese laid out for everyone.

Elliot moved around, as if he wanted to organize everybody, but it was his wife, Sidney, who pulled him down to sit, while Trace glared at him as if he'd beat Elliot's ass if the guy got up again. And from the way Elliot blushed, he'd probably like that. And that was something I really didn't want to know about my cousin.

They were all happily settled, everybody married, ready to start the next phase of their lives. And when I had first moved here, I had felt almost on the outside looking in, watching a life I could have had that had slipped through my fingers.

But now it was mine as well. I didn't have to beg and ask any longer.

It could be mine.

Aurora slid her fingers into mine, as Wyatt and Gabriel came through, a guitar in Gabriel's hand, and a case of booze in Wyatt's.

"Excuse me, this is wine country," Elijah said so primly that I had to snort.

"Well, we also have liquor. Imagine that."

"I'm here for the liquor," Elliot said, and Trace murmured something in his ear that I knew had to be a dirty joke when Sidney blushed and slapped Trace on the shoulder, and everybody laughed.

Brooks came in last, looking around at everyone quietly before smiling softly, and taking a seat next to Eli and Alexis. Aurora and I found seats by Lark, and then we were all eating and laughing, and I honestly couldn't believe that this was my life.

Everything had started with a lost dress, and the loss of something more. But we had found our way out of the darkness, and I had to remember that every moment was precious. Every moment meant something.

You had to hold on to those moments. Hold on to those pieces. And then someday you could puzzle them together to figure out who you were and what you craved.

With Aurora at my side, blending in with my family like she had always been there, I knew that final puzzle piece had made its way in. There might be a few more along the way—in fact I knew there probably would be, but this was where we could settle. Where we could build our foundation.

And I would be forever grateful for that lost dress, and for the strength it took for the woman that I loved to give hers up.

The memories we made in this room and on this retreat would be forever ingrained on my soul. And I knew I was one lucky bastard.

Wyatt tilted his wine glass at me, I did the same with my mixed drink that he had made, and I smiled, knowing that this was a beginning, not an ending.

This was a moment. And I couldn't wait for the next.

CHAPTER NINETEEN
WYATT

As the final customer left, I waved them goodbye and locked up behind them. It had been a long day, and this wasn't exactly where I had thought I would be in terms of my life, but it was good. I was with family, I was serving beer, Wilder wine, and Wilder Vodka. I hadn't even realized that this was my purpose in life, but then again, a master's degree in chemistry didn't get you much these days. To get a good job, you needed a PhD, or some other discipline, but I had been forced to get out of school a bit early thanks to Isabelle. I scowled at that thought, annoyed with myself. Hell, that was wrong of me. I couldn't blame my ex-wife for everything. Or, well, isn't, ex-wife, ex-wife. I just needed her to sign the final divorce papers and then she would be out of my hair forever.

That was why I had started over. To get her out of my life and get on with whatever I was supposed to do now.

Because I had been the one who decided to get out of grad school early so I could get a full-time job and start our future.

Life never really turned out the way it was supposed to, but then again, my brothers were evidence of that. Just look at how Ridge was starting his new life, changing the score, and yet he had hid everything from us.

I wasn't any better. Only my brothers knew I had been married. Or fuck, was *still* married. I rubbed my temples, once again annoyed with myself for letting my thoughts go down that path. I just wanted to get this over with. But Isabelle currently had the papers, so the ball was in her court now.

I went back to closing up shop, cleaning up everything. I was the last one here, as I had already sent my staff home. It usually took two people to close out; I didn't allow my staff to close up solo. But since it was me and I owned the damn place, I was fine doing it on my own, as any mistake made would be on me.

I had already put the bank bag away, emptied the till, and cleaned the bar area, now I just wanted one more quick run-through, and I would head home.

There was a family dinner the next evening, which was still odd for me, but I didn't mind it. It was nice to be around people who actually wanted me there, instead of people who hated me on sight.

I was whistling a tune I had heard all night over the speakers when it was as if I had summoned the devil herself.

I looked through the glass doors at her quick sharp knock, and glared.

Resigned, I knew I couldn't hide from her. Plus, I didn't want her to have the fucking satisfaction. So I went to the front door and unlocked it.

"Do you like keeping me waiting?" Isabelle asked, that shrill voice new. She'd always been soft and kind. Maybe demanding, but hell, I was just as demanding if you asked her. Maybe that was just what happened when you looked through the lens of people who not only didn't love each other anymore, but actively hated each other.

"Didn't even hear you outside. We're closed now, Isabelle."

"Yes, your little bar. How quaint." She looked around the place, and I wasn't sure if she was really seeing it, or wondering what she should get of it. The problem was, the divorce papers weren't final. If she wanted to, she could take me back to court and try to take this.

That's why I had put this in a family trust, and I wasn't the sole owner. I had done what I could to protect my family and to protect this place. I just had to hope it was enough. That Isabelle was as tired of me as much as I was of her, and wanted this to be done already.

"I'd ask if there's something I could do for you, but you always want something and I'm not in the mood."

"You're such an asshole."

"Maybe. But I learned from the best."

"Oh, shut up. I'm here to do something that you've always wanted."

"Yeah?" I asked, my heart racing. I needed her to just sign the papers. To go away. I needed to start over.

"Well, I figured it was time. Now that I've gotten what I wanted."

I narrowed my gaze. "What's that?"

"Someone better than you. Right, baby?"

Aaron walked through the door then, his broad shoulders taking up most of the doorway. He had that familiar scowl on his face, over the chiseled jaw that had always made all the girls around us swoon. He had been my best friend. My confidant, and now he stood with my hopefully soon-to-be ex-wife. One of the many reasons I wanted that divorce.

"What are you doing here?" I asked, keeping my voice as neutral as possible.

"I'm making sure that my woman's safe. Never quite sure in a bar like this. I mean come on, a bar?"

"If you guys are just here to bullshit, you can leave now. I have to close up."

"Oh, so you're closed, that's why nobody's here."

"You can't belittle me. I'm over it."

A lie, but I could fake it.

"Whatever you say," Isabelle said, before she snapped her fingers at Aaron. Aaron, the dutiful boyfriend, lover, cheat, slid papers out of his back pocket.

"Here you go, love."

"Thank you, boo." She shoved the papers towards me. "Signed and delivered. I sent a copy to my lawyer, and you can do whatever the fuck you want with this one. But it's over now. We're officially divorced. I'm done. Now I get what I want." She waved her fingers at me, the shining diamond on her left ring finger sparkling under the bar lights.

I thought I would've felt a little more. A little something. But there was nothing.

My ex-wife, *finally* my ex-wife, was officially marrying my dumbass ex-best friend. That made sense.

"I'd say congratulations, but I really don't give a fuck about you two. Thank you for the papers. Now get out."

"You really are a jealous asshole," Aaron put in.

"I don't know what I saw in you."

"You liked my dick and my bank account, that's all I really remember," I said casually.

She narrowed her gaze at me, while Aaron's face just reddened in anger.

"Seriously. Both of you get out. We're done here."

"You're acting just like Ava," Aaron spat. "You're a little petty bitch just like she is."

"Considering you cheated on Ava just like Isabelle cheated on me, I'm not sure what you mean."

"It's not cheating if it's love," Isabelle purred as she looked over at her new man, and I barely resisted the urge to throw up.

"We're done here," I repeated. "Get out. Ava and I are pretty much winning with this."

Aaron stopped. "My ex is such a bitch, and she can't handle life without me. You'd know if you ever spoke to her. But she hates your guts as much as she hates mine. Works pretty well for me, don't you think?"

And with that, he gave me a two-finger salute and

Isabelle hooked her arm around his waist before they sauntered out, leaving me alone with the divorce papers and a heavy heart.

Because while I had my family, my bar, Ava had something else. Faith. Her daughter with Aaron. The little girl that Aaron left behind when he and Isabelle decided to blow up all of our lives.

But Ava hated me, and frankly, we had never gotten along. The fact that our exes had cheated on us with each other just meant that we would always butt heads. The only thing we had in common was the fact that we had horrible taste. But I still felt for Faith. There was just no way where it would make sense for me to help them out. Not that Ava would ever take help.

She was better off without Aaron, Isabelle, and me in her life.

I shook my head and slid the divorce papers into my bag, figuring it was time to get home. I'd had a long day, and things had been looking up, but now they just tasted sour.

I turned at the scuff of a boot as something came at my head, and I lifted my arm up, trying to block the blow. But whatever it was, was hard and heavy and stars shattered behind my eyes as I hit the ground, gasping for air. A boot kicked me in the gut, then caught me again in the hip before it slammed onto my shoulder, and I heard someone trying to get to the till, and to the extra bank bag I had in my bag.

I tried to get up, tried to say anything, but there was nothing, just another boot to the kidney, and then darkness.

NEXT IN THE WILDER BROTHERS SERIES:
Wyatt and Ava make a choice in FOREVER FOR US.

IF YOU'D LIKE TO READ A BONUS SCENE FEATURING AURORA
& RIDGE:
CHECK OUT THIS SPECIAL EPILOGUE!

A NOTE FROM CARRIE
ANN RYAN

Thank you so much for reading MOMENTS FOR YOU.

If you couldn't tell, this book was personal to me. I ended up writing a vital scene on the anniversary of my husband's death and in doing so, I knew my characters were feeling the same moments. In the end, I'm so proud of this book and the introduction of the Wilder Cousins.

Ridge and Aurora's romance wasn't easy, but nothing worthwhile is. I also craved cake SO MUCH during this book that it bled over into the next novella!

Naomi and Amos FINALLY get their story in A Wilder Wedding! And then you get to see exactly what Wyatt is up to in Forever For Us!

The Wilder Brothers Series:

Book 1: One Way Back to Me

Book 2: Always the One for Me

Book 3: The Path to You

Book 4: Coming Home for Us

Book 5: Stay Here With Me

Book 6: Finding the Road to Us

Book 7: Moments for You

Book 7.5: A Wilder Wedding

Book 8: Forever For Us

NEXT IN THE WILDER BROTHERS SERIES:
Wyatt and Ava make a choice in FOREVER FOR US.

IF YOU'D LIKE TO READ A BONUS SCENE FEATURING AURORA
& RIDGE:
CHECK OUT THIS SPECIAL EPILOGUE!

If you want to make sure you know what's coming next from me, you can sign up for my newsletter at www. CarrieAnnRyan.com; follow me on twitter at @CarrieAnnRyan, or like my Facebook page. I also have a Facebook Fan Club where we have trivia, chats, and other goodies. You guys are the reason I get to do what I do and I thank you.

Make sure you're signed up for my MAILING LIST so you can know when the next releases are available as well as find giveaways and FREE READS.

Happy Reading!

ALSO FROM CARRIE ANN RYAN

The Montgomery Ink Legacy Series:

Book 1: Bittersweet Promises

Book 2: At First Meet

Book 2.5: Happily Ever Never

Book 3: Longtime Crush

Book 4: Best Friend Temptation

Book 4.5: Happily Ever Maybe

Book 5: Last First Kiss

Book 6: His Second Chance

Book 7: One Night with You

The Wilder Brothers Series:

Book 1: One Way Back to Me

Book 2: Always the One for Me

Book 3: The Path to You

Book 4: Coming Home for Us

Book 5: Stay Here With Me

Book 6: Finding the Road to Us

Book 7: Moments for You

Book 7.5: A Wilder Wedding

Book 8: Forever For Us

The First Time Series:

Book 1: Good Time Boyfriend

Book 2: Last Minute Fiancé

Book 3: Second Chance Husband

The Aspen Pack Series:

Book 1: Etched in Honor

Book 2: Hunted in Darkness

Book 3: Mated in Chaos

Book 4: Harbored in Silence

Book 5: Marked in Flames

The Montgomery Ink: Fort Collins Series:

Book 1: Inked Persuasion

Book 2: Inked Obsession

Book 3: Inked Devotion

Book 3.5: Nothing But Ink

Book 4: Inked Craving

Book 5: Inked Temptation

The Montgomery Ink: Boulder Series:

Book 1: Wrapped in Ink

Book 2: Sated in Ink

Book 3: Embraced in Ink

Book 3: Moments in Ink

Book 4: Seduced in Ink

Book 4.5: Captured in Ink

Book 4.7: Inked Fantasy

Book 4.8: A Very Montgomery Christmas

Montgomery Ink: Colorado Springs

Book 1: Fallen Ink

Book 2: Restless Ink

Book 2.5: Ashes to Ink

Book 3: Jagged Ink

Book 3.5: Ink by Numbers

Montgomery Ink Denver:

Book 0.5: Ink Inspired

Book 0.6: Ink Reunited

Book 1: Delicate Ink

Book 1.5: Forever Ink

Book 2: Tempting Boundaries

Book 3: Harder than Words

Book 3.5: Finally Found You

Book 4: Written in Ink

Book 4.5: <u>Hidden Ink</u>

Book 5: <u>Ink Enduring</u>

Book 6: <u>Ink Exposed</u>

Book 6.5: <u>Adoring Ink</u>

Book 6.6: <u>Love, Honor, & Ink</u>

Book 7: <u>Inked Expressions</u>

Book 7.3: <u>Dropout</u>

Book 7.5: <u>Executive Ink</u>

Book 8: <u>Inked Memories</u>

Book 8.5: <u>Inked Nights</u>

Book 8.7: <u>Second Chance Ink</u>

Book 8.5: Montgomery Midnight Kisses

Bonus: Inked Kingdom

The On My Own Series:

Book 0.5: My First Glance

Book 1: My One Night

Book 2: My Rebound

Book 3: My Next Play

Book 4: My Bad Decisions

The Promise Me Series:

Book 1: Forever Only Once

Book 2: From That Moment

Book 3: Far From Destined

Book 4: From Our First

The Less Than Series:

Book 1: Breathless With Her

Book 2: Reckless With You

Book 3: Shameless With Him

The Fractured Connections Series:

Book 1: Breaking Without You

Book 2: Shouldn't Have You

Book 3: Falling With You

Book 4: Taken With You

The Whiskey and Lies Series:

Book 1: Whiskey Secrets

Book 2: Whiskey Reveals

Book 3: Whiskey Undone

The Gallagher Brothers Series:

Book 1: Love Restored

Book 2: Passion Restored

Book 3: Hope Restored

The Ravenwood Coven Series:

Book 1: Dawn Unearthed

Book 2: Dusk Unveiled

Book 3: Evernight Unleashed

The Talon Pack:

Book 1: <u>Tattered Loyalties</u>

Book 2: <u>An Alpha's Choice</u>

Book 3: <u>Mated in Mist</u>

Book 4: <u>Wolf Betrayed</u>

Book 5: <u>Fractured Silence</u>

Book 6: <u>Destiny Disgraced</u>

Book 7: <u>Eternal Mourning</u>

Book 8: <u>Strength Enduring</u>

Book 9: <u>Forever Broken</u>

Book 10: Mated in Darkness

Book 11: Fated in Winter

Redwood Pack Series:

Book 1: <u>An Alpha's Path</u>

Book 2: <u>A Taste for a Mate</u>

Book 3: <u>Trinity Bound</u>

Book 3.5: <u>A Night Away</u>

Book 4: <u>Enforcer's Redemption</u>

Book 4.5: <u>Blurred Expectations</u>

Book 4.7: <u>Forgiveness</u>

Book 5: <u>Shattered Emotions</u>

Book 6: <u>Hidden Destiny</u>

Book 6.5: <u>A Beta's Haven</u>

Book 7: <u>Fighting Fate</u>

Book 7.5: <u>Loving the Omega</u>

Book 7.7: <u>The Hunted Heart</u>

Book 8: <u>Wicked Wolf</u>

The Elements of Five Series:

Book 1: From Breath and Ruin

Book 2: From Flame and Ash

Book 3: From Spirit and Binding

Book 4: From Shadow and Silence

Dante's Circle Series:

Book 1: <u>Dust of My Wings</u>

Book 2: <u>Her Warriors' Three Wishes</u>

Book 3: <u>An Unlucky Moon</u>

Book 3.5: <u>His Choice</u>

Book 4: <u>Tangled Innocence</u>

Book 5: <u>Fierce Enchantment</u>

Book 6: <u>An Immortal's Song</u>

Book 7: <u>Prowled Darkness</u>

Book 8: Dante's Circle Reborn

Holiday, Montana Series:

Book 1: <u>Charmed Spirits</u>

Book 2: <u>Santa's Executive</u>

Book 3: <u>Finding Abigail</u>

Book 4: <u>Her Lucky Love</u>

Book 5: Dreams of Ivory

The Branded Pack Series:
   (Written with Alexandra Ivy)
   Book 1: <u>Stolen and Forgiven</u>
   Book 2: <u>Abandoned and Unseen</u>
   Book 3: <u>Buried and Shadowed</u>

ABOUT THE AUTHOR

Carrie Ann Ryan is the New York Times and USA Today bestselling author of contemporary, paranormal, and young adult romance. Her works include the Montgomery Ink, Redwood Pack, Fractured Connections, and Elements of Five series, which have sold over 3.0 million books worldwide. She started writing while in graduate school for her advanced degree in chemistry and hasn't stopped since. Carrie Ann has written over seventy-five novels and novellas with more in the works. When she's not losing herself in her emotional and action-packed worlds, she's reading as much as she can while wrangling her clowder of cats who have more followers than she does.

www.CarrieAnnRyan.com